The Revenge
Of
Sherlock Holmes

Phil Growick

Paperback ISBN 9781780925189
ePub ISBN 9781780925196
PDF ISBN 9781780925202

Published in the UK by MX Publishing
335 Princess Park Manor, Royal Drive,
London, N11 3GX
www.mxpublishing.com

Cover design by www.staunch.com

This is for Bennett

And Maiju, always Maiju

Contents

AUTHOR'S NOTE

Many of the characters in this book are historical personages. In this narrative, as well as in history, all were as described herein. However, I've taken certain license with timeframe and characters' ages.

A note about particular Americans, however, is needed. While most of the world may not be familiar with Lucky Luciano, Meyer Lansky, Bugsy Siegel or Arnold Rothstein, these men, founders of what would become organized crime in America, have, through books, movies and time, achieved the mythos akin to Britain's Robin Hood.

But these men robbed from rich and poor alike, killed and organized crime on a global scale.

A further word, though this about their unique speech patterns. These men were children of recent European immigrants, or immigrants themselves. They spoke the English of the New York City streets; more harsh and hurried than we might wish.

In their speech, they frequently dropped the "g" at the end of any verb, and seemed to forget that the word "to" had an "o" attached; so that the words would flow as in "I'm goin' t' the bar."; and is written as such.

One advantage of their speech was that more educated individuals might mistake their guttural utterances as a sign of lower intelligence; which, in many instances, was a fatal mistake.

It was not a foreign language they were speaking; just lower East Side Manhattan English, circa 1920. And the ethnic slurs they slung at members of any group other than their own, were the norm of the streets at that time. Bullets and bigotry.

Finally, a certain event, herein, may prove evocative of the motion picture, *The Godfather*. In this narrative, however, the event and the people involved are portrayed as it actually happened.

HISTORICAL CARACTERS

BRITISH
Sidney Reilly, SIS (Secret Intelligence Service), Master Spy.
David Lloyd George, Former Prime Minister of England.
Winston Churchill, former First Lord of the Admiralty.

RUSSIAN
The Romanovs, The Imperial Russian Family.
Vladmir Illyich Lenin, Leader of the Bolsheviks.
Leon Trostky, Commander of the Bolshevik Red Army.
Stalin, Enemy of Trotsky and a rising Bolshevik.

AMERICAN
Charles "Lucky" Luciano and Meyer Lansky, The men who organized crime in the United States.
Benjamin "Bugsy" Siegel, The closest mobster associate of Luciano and Lansky.
Al Capone, The gangland boss of Chicago.
Salvatore Maranzano and Guiseppe Masseria, the bosses who started the Castellammarese War in New York City.
Legs Diamond, Dutch Schultz, Kid Twsit Reles, Lepke Buchhalter, young mobsters who helped Luciano, Lansky and Siegel.
Mary Pickford and Douglas Fairbanks, Hollywood royalty.

Preface

Although I introduced myself when *The Secret Journal of Dr. Watson,* was first published, I thought it best to do it again.

I'm Dr. John Watson, the grandson of the more illustrious bearer of that name; the man who not only chronicled the adventures of Sherlock Holmes, but was his invaluable colleague and dearest friend.

It's been about a year since *The Secret Journal of Dr. Watson* was published, back in September of 1994; a year that's not only changed my and my family's lives, but has changed history with a venal velocity I wasn't prepared for.

None of us privy to the contents of that journal, except for my grandfather, its author, were prepared. His warnings to me are right there in that journal.

Unless you've been living in a cave or under a rock or out in the outback, I'm not sure that you still wouldn't have heard the outcry. And if you haven't read or heard about my grandfather's secret journal, here's a very brief synopsis; although it might be wise if you read *The Secret Journal of Dr. Watson* before beginning this:

In June of 1918, as WWI dragged on and the Russian Revolution wasn't even one year past, King George V and the serving Prime Minster, David Lloyd George, asked Sherlock Holmes to go into Russia and rescue the Romanovs, the Russian Royal family; close cousins to the King and under orders of execution by the Bolsheviks. This request was made in the most confidential manner, of course.

My grandfather had to accompany Holmes because the Tsarevich Alexi was a haemophiliac and would need constant medical attention. Holmes was told he would be met by special people in Russia, already in place, who would help him with the rescue. The most of important of these special people was Sidney Reilly, SIS, master spy.

But as Holmes and my grandfather soon learned, they were not sure who to trust with their lives, much less that of the Romanovs. All this led to the subsequent death of Holmes by the Germans and the chronicle my grandfather wrote describing Holmes' heroic last adventure, in service to his King and country.

All epic deceit.

Because of world veneration of Sherlock Holmes and my grandfather, and my grandfather's revelations in his secret journal about the truth of Holmes' death and the rescue of the Imperial Romanovs, the British government came under intense global, political attack.

And who could blame the world? Certainly I wouldn't. I'm the one who gave the journal over for publication, positive that it did not offend The Official Secrets Act of 1911. I'm the one who was the first to be so shocked and outraged.

But this is now and that was then and therein lays the continuing problem. Because what happened then, if it's all true, and which, of course, I believe it wholeheartedly to be, may shape current world events in ways we can't even imagine.

For instance: if there are legitimate direct royal Romanov claimants to the throne of Russia, given that deflated behemoth's ongoing internal problems, couldn't this further destabilize the delicate political and social fabric there, so precarious already?

Then what would happen should Russia fragment further? But I'd rather not dwell on that here. In fact, I shiver at the thought. Funny, it seems that we need a stable Russia now, just as we did back then. The more things change, etc.

But I have a different story to tell. A continuation of the bizarre events of my grandfather's secret journal; answers to the questions I put forward at the end of that journal, and that the whole world has been asking me to answer ever since.

My word, is there any among you who have not seen me on the pages of your daily newspapers, or in the magazines, or on the TV chat shows, or heard me on the radio?

I've been interviewed and written about by so many people with such varied agendas that I've virtually given up my practice and devoted this past year to speaking about my grandfather's journal.

The monies or stipends received, except for expenses, have all been donated to various recognised charities; as has been attested to by the various and sundry media. If you ask how my wife, Joan, and our sons were to live, I already had money saved as a successful physician and from a comfortable inheritance from Joan's father's business; which had been sold upon his death in 1980.

And I most certainly have not uttered one syllable about the answers to the questions the journal raised.

Until now.

Also, for the past year the whole world has also been trying to discover the incognito identity of Sidney Romanov-Reilly. But to no avail. Only I know who he is, although I don't know where he is, nor how to contact him. He's always contacted me and I've not heard from him since a few days after our first meeting.

In fact, one of the conditions of me learning about what happened to Holmes and the Romanovs and Clay and the others, was that I wouldn't disclose this information until one year had passed after the journal's publication. One year for the world to digest the material, acquire acute dyspepsia from it, recover, and then, when things had sorted themselves out, sort of, the final revelations were to be divulged; which would probably start the process all over again.

And this time, with new people added to the mystery; as seemingly disparate and disconnected as Winston Churchill, Babe Ruth, Al Capone and Lenin.

Sidney, Again

I'll begin on the afternoon of August 11, 1993; after Sidney and I first met early that morning and when he said he would come round to pick me up and to give me all the answers to all the questions.

At precisely two p.m., Joan told me there was a rather large man at the door. He was dressed as a chauffeur and she wanted to know who he was and what he wanted with me.

Please remember that Joan knew nothing of the incredible events of the previous night, when I first read my grandfather's secret journal, and therefore was only asking a concerned and logical question. I did what any other long-married husband would do with earth-shaking secrets to hide: I played for time and tore the truth.

"Oh, didn't I tell you? One of my patients has sent him around to fetch me to him because he's too ill to come in to see me." I'm sure I was trying to be so matter-of-fact that I didn't convince her one jot.

"Really? Which patient?"

"Why, uh, Mr. Smith, yes, Mr. Smith." God, couldn't I have come up with something a tad more inventive?

"I've never heard you mention a Mr. Smith before," she said, with her right eyebrow arched so high it met her hairline.

Joan had that wife's intuition about a husband when she perceives there's a fib
floating about. She's far more intelligent than I and a few years older, which seems to have given her the wisdom of the ages.

"Well, uh, he's a new patient, a new patient. Very ill, very ill."

I realized I was repeating everything I said and perspiring at an alarming rate,
soaking my clothing for all to see. I raced towards the door.

"What's wrong with him, John?"

"Uh, Fraggums's Disease, terrible, terrible. Bye." I slammed the door behind me, breathed hard and let the chauffeur lead the way.

This time, there was no Rolls, as in the morning. This time, the chauffeur held open the door to a large brown Mercedes limo. There sat Sidney, who gestured me in.

"How many of these things do you own?" I asked as I sat.

"Not important. Merely a conveyance."

Only on much later reflection did I realize that Sidney's words were not a direct answer to my question, but rather a mere statement. However, once in and with Sidney greeting me warmly, the car began moving with no instruction from him.

"So how did you sleep?" he asked.

"How do you think?"

He laughed.

"Well, my friend, I'm afraid you're going to have many more nights akin to the last one. We'll simply drive, and oh, yes..."

With that, he reached into his right suit jacket pocket and pulled out a black cloth.

"John, you'll indulge if you don't mind, but please..."

He gestured for me to put on the blindfold.

"You're serious?"

"I'm afraid so, John. You see, we're going to my home and while you may know who I am, but not really, there are few others who do. Therefore I don't want you to know where I live or how to get there. Perhaps one day."

"Well why can't we just go sit at a pub or club and you can continue where you left off."

"Ah, if it were only that easy. Though these kinds of things never are…"

I wondered what he meant by that.

"John, there's something I must show you to help move things along. But it's at my home and much too precious for me to carry with me."

"Ah," I thought, "he's going to show me the Romanov crown jewels." He held the cloth towards me again. This time, however, his face showed an expression that removed all doubt as to what I must do. So, I did.

"Good, good. No peeking now." He laughed, again.

"We'll be there in no time, and if you don't mind, I'd rather we just keep still until we arrive." Which we did, but I don't know how long the ride was because he also removed my watch as I sat there, so I couldn't get a judge on time. Oh, he was clever all right. The old Sidney Reilly DNA was very alive and well with this Sidney, his son.

In good time our car stopped and, I believe, I was led into the house by the chauffeur or another domestic; but it was Sidney's voice I heard saying, "There's a step coming up, be careful, that's it. Good."

Then I heard him say, "You may remove the blindfold now;" which I did instantaneously.

The first thing I saw when I removed the cloth was Sidney standing in front of me, smiling. It was the first time I'd actually seen him full length, so-to-speak, and I hadn't thought about his height before. But he was tall, about six-feet, I'd say, and very trim. And very erect. Well, he was a Romanov. Watered down, perhaps, but nonetheless.

The next thing I noticed was the room in which we stood. It was something out of one of those *War and Peace* type palaces, but smack in the middle of London. Ornate was an understatement. Gold leaf was everywhere; on the cherubs adorning the crown molding, on the edges of the richly decorated ebony furniture, on the Nubian lamps.

The floors were the most beautifully polished woods I'd ever seen, with intricate geometric inlays. And though I didn't look up, I saw, from a gilded mirror, that I was standing under the most gigantic gold and crystal chandelier one could imagine. I'd never been to Buckingham Palace, but I'd easily wager this room would not go begging in comparison to any room there.

As we stood and Sidney waited and watched my reactions, he finally spoke.

"Now, it may be difficult, John, but please try to follow me."

"All right."

"Good. What you're about to learn may be even more unbelievable than what you read in your grandfather's journal last night."

Were I not a doctor I would've sworn that my heart stopped beating, albeit only momentarily.

"What you will now learn was also told to me by my father, who was told by Sherlock Holmes; although both my father and Holmes' stories intertwined at various times and each needed the other to fill out the complete facts of each other's stories; but without your grandfather knowing anything about either; except when he and your grandmother were directly involved."

He must've seen the look of utter bewilderment on my face, because what he just said made as much sense as someone speaking colloquial Saturnian.

He laughed.

"Yes, yes; I can see how that might sound confusing, but I assure you, it'll all make sense shortly."

"And how is that to happen when I didn't understand one thing you just said?"

"Very easily. I'll let your grandfather tell you."

At that, I'm positive my face must've born such an expression of utter astonishment that I literally had to force my mouth shut for fear of trapping flies.

"Yes, quite. Just follow me," he said.

He was still laughing gently to himself, enjoying his joke immensely, as I followed him to an adjoining room. He opened a double door revealing a magnificent, ancient-oak-lined study. And there, on the most ornately carved mahogany desk you could imagine, sat an exquisitely bound, deep burgundy leather volume, with gold tooling around the edges.

His hand made a circular motion gesturing for me to go round and see what the volume was. This I did immediately while my peripheral vision picked up what I perceived to be Romanov family photos in various silver frames on floor-to-ceiling, overstuffed bookshelves and on bric-a-brac jammed tables throughout the study.

I gazed down on the cover of the volume and stopped where I stood. It had the familiar three letters: JHW.

And then I heard Sidney's words.

"Prepare yourself, John. What you see before you is your grandfather's retelling of all he learned subsequent to his penning of his secret journal, based upon what I was trying to explain to you just now. I simply had his pages encased in something beautiful, as they deserved to be. Of course I've already read everything; just in case I felt particular events should be excised. One must preserve family secrets; even from you."

He pulled out the chair tucked tightly in the desk and I quite literally fell into it,
sitting there transfixed as I stared at the initials.

"You can open it, John. It won't bite you. And then again, it most certainly might. I'll leave you two alone. I have a suspicion that I won't be seeing you again for quite some time.

"Oh, yes, I've also had the clocks removed from this room as a further precaution of what time it is right now. When you've finished, I'll return your watch. Though you might want a better one." Then that Sidney laugh again as he left the room, closing the door behind him.

I was too dazed to answer, to speak, to make any kind of utterance whatsoever. My heart was racing so fast that I took my own pulse and forced myself to calm down.

If what Sidney had said was true, and in my heart I knew that it was, I also knew that I was now going to become privy to events known only to a very few people.

Then I reached for the cover, opened it, and began to read words handwritten by grandfather so very long ago. However, the chapter titles were not his. I've added them to make his disclosures easier to follow in his labyrinthine tale.

But not, necessarily, easier to fathom.

My Grandfather Begins

What I am about to divulge, I almost cannot believe myself; although my wife, Elizabeth, and I, actually took part in some of the unfortunate events recounted herein.

After all that I had lived through with the Romanovs and Reilly and Holmes, and detailed in my journal, these events were even more fantastic and unbelievable; if that were at all possible.

Unlike my journal, the events will not be told in chronological order, because many of these disparate events were happening concurrently. So please forgive the occasional leap from one tale focused on one individual or event to another. I hope you understand and will not find it too jarring.

I must admit, as a literary device, I find it rather intriguing.

I also caution you that this is most certainly not one of my usual Holmes tales, where he uses his prodigious powers of intellect and deduction to solve a grave mystery; although there are enough layers upon layers of historical intertwining and involvement of many famous, and infamous, historical personages to give one a migraine trying to weave this twine into a logical fabric.

Except for what Elizabeth and I personally experienced, all that I now commit to these pages were conveyed to me by Sidney Reilly himself, in my home in London, on four separate occasions; and in one final letter and package, well subsequent to our final meeting.

After all that he and I had been through together, I had absolutely no reason to doubt one word of what he told me.

Yet, as Holmes had made me so astutely aware, how much of what Reilly said was truth, and how much was fecund fabrication?

Though Reilly would much later tell me of what happened to Holmes, told to him by Holmes himself when they met much later in the history of these events, in our first meeting at my home in London, he knew nothing of Holmes' fate. Therefore, he spoke only of what happened to himself, subsequent to his taking leave of us in Russia; in itself an absolutely incredible accumulation of astounding adventures.

It would not be until our second meeting at my home that Reilly told of Holmes' fate. But since this narrative may prove beyond intricate, I've taken the liberty of melding what Reilly told me of Holmes directly into the chronology; as though he had told of the events during our first meeting.

This only sounds confusing, but as you continue, my account will become easier to comprehend.

What you will now read, for the most part, is a retelling of a tale previously told by someone to someone else expert in tailoring tales to his taste; which, in itself, is a sentence needing elucidation by Holmes.

But I trust my own elucidation should suffice: I will be telling you what Reilly told me that Holmes told him. Who, then, can you believe?

In these pages, I have decided to believe Reilly; perhaps because I need to believe Reilly. It will be up to you to decide what you choose to believe.

In that regard, much of these pages deal with Holmes in America, or, to be more precise, in New York City. For there, as hard as it will be to fathom, Holmes became an important part of America's nascent organized crime world. In fact, he became one of its founding fathers, if I may adopt that familiar Yankee term.

You will now learn what happened to Reilly, to the Romanovs collectively and individually, to young Yardley and all the others whose acquaintances you met in my secret journal. But most of all, you will learn what happened to Holmes.

Therefore, I will begin with what Reilly told me about Holmes' rescue.

Holmes Rescued

"Sharks. Sharks."

These were the words Holmes was muttering over and over, his rescuers said. But of course, they didn't know the man they'd saved was Holmes. They didn't know who he was, or what he was, he just was; and that was good enough for them for the moment.

By the look of him, he had been out there for days. He was dehydrated, sunburned badly and delirious. But that was because of the all of the above, plus a surfeit of swallowed seawater.

It was lucky that he was found adrift in that lifeboat. But from which ship? There was no ship's name on the lifeboat. Another mystery.

In Port Royal, South Carolina, the United States, where he now was, he would be nursed back to health by the family who found him. Then the questions would be answered.

When he first opened his eyes, two days after Hank, Lou, and Martin Curtis found him, he wanted to know where he was and when it was.

He was told it was August 18, 1918, and that he'd been picked up two days previously. But they didn't know how long he'd been out there. They were on their usual fishing run when they happened to see him. Then Hank told him what he'd been repeating when he was hauled aboard their little scow, "Laughing Abby", after Hank's wife, and Martin and Lou's mother, Abigail.

Hank later remarked, when Holmes was well enough to be human again, that when Homes heard the words he'd been repeating in his delirium, Holmes' eyes flashed open so violently Hank thought both would go popping out and rolling about the floor like the marbles Lou and Martin had played with as young boys.

Holmes remembered: he had been with Captain Yardley, having a comforting nightcap and the next thing he knew, he was here. It was as if a child had suddenly realized his father had just tried to kill him.

Holmes knew what this meant. He had been the victim of attempted murder; and he suspected who was behind it. But if that were so, what of Watson? Was he safe? Had he met with some similar perfidy? And the Romanovs? What of them?

In that instant, Holmes realized that to survive, he must cease being Sherlock Holmes and become one of the pseudo-selves he'd established decades ago; for Holmes always suspected the need to take shelter out of his own identity would come one day.

This was the day.

He surveyed the man who saved him. He looked to be about fifty or so, tall and lithe and giving off the feeling of a tremendous tensile strength. He had a benign face with an easy smile. But it was his eyes that Holmes realized were surveying him as intently as he surveyed Curtis.

"Thank you for saving me."

"Well, you can thank the Almighty and my son Martin's eagle eye. He saw ya first and his kid brother, Lou, grabbed ya first. I just cut the engine and let the boys haul ya aboard. You're in Lou's bed right now. He figured ya needed it more than him.

"And if ya have a mind to know where that bed happens to be, it happens to be in Port Royal, South Carolina. I hope we're not too far from where you were headed. Which I gotta ask about because ya been laid up here for two days. We did some checkin' and we couldn't find no note of no vessel goin' down nowhere. Nowhere.

"And we all know ya weren't dropped down from heaven, and now that I listened to ya I know you ain't American. So how the hell didya get where ya were? Where'd ya come from? Where were ya goin'? And who the hell are ya? If you don't mind me askin' and if you have the strength to be answerin'?"

Holmes had only the strength to smile at the outburst of fact and questions shot at him and marveled at how true it was about Americans: they will tell you their whole life story fifteen seconds after they've met you and expect the same from you immediately thereafter.

Since this particular American and his sons had been good enough to save his life, answers were the least he could supply in return; even if they weren't the truth.

In addition, what puzzled and concerned him was that he was in South Carolina. Why would a simple fishing scow be so far from its home waters? But since he seemed to be in caring hands, he continued with his own masquerade.

"What, what day is it, pray tell?"

"August seventeenth by the calendar on that wall."

"Thank you. My name is Hamilton. James Hamilton."

"How ya doin', Jim ?"

"Jim? Oh, yes. Fine, thanks to you, I believe; and your sons."

"No, Abby's been the one really carin' for ya. She's been the one feedin' ya and wipin' yer head and all. We kinda know how t' take care of ourselves. And each other."

"I must thank her, then."

"Abby's in town. She'll be back later. The boys went back to their real job. But you were goin' to answer those questions I asked; and here ya are askin' me more questions than I'm askin' you. We're all as curious as Pandora about you."

"I'm originally from London."

"I thought you were a Limey, uh, sorry, British, when ya opened yer mouth."

"No offense taken. I was a professor at the Royal Oceanographic Institute on Bermuda. Ichthyology. I must let them know I'm safe."

Holmes was testing Curtis. After all, Curtis had just made mention of Pandora, and, usually, simple fishermen have little need or knowledge of Greek mythology. Not even if they're Greek. And his speech pattern was almost as if he was trying to speak English improperly; to give the impression of a coastal yokel. It seemed they were not merely indigenous to England, after all.

"Ichthyologist? So you're a fisherman, too?" Curtis had to laugh at his own joke. He had also just passed, or failed, the test. Holmes was not, as yet, sure which.

"Yes, I suppose so. Very droll, indeed."

"But how'd ya come to be floatin' out there?"

"I was on a day outing and I hate to admit it, being a son of a seafaring nation and an ichthyologist to boot, but I couldn't handle my little boat very well and somehow I was pitched overboard.

"I must have hit my head on the boat, swallowed enough seawater to quench the thirst of Thetis, then somehow found the strength of drag myself back on the boat, where I surmise, I passed out." Holmes noticed that Curtis made no inquiry as to the identity of Thethis.

"And ya weren't with nobody?"

"Just myself. Foolish,what?"

"If you weren't so fragile, friend, stupid is what I'd call it. But I guess you've learned your lesson."

"Yes, ironic. As a teacher I'm still learning." Curtis saw that Holmes was still in need of sleep. His energy was waning.

"Yeah, well. I'll leave ya alone now to rest some more. Abby and I will check in on ya later. And if ya need anythin', of course just holler."

"Thank you, again."

"Don't mention it." Curtis closed the door behind him.

Alone in these strange, yet seemingly safe, surroundings, Holmes worried about the fate of Watson, Reilly, the Romanovs and the rest. If he had been the target of assassination, what had happened to them? Were they alive, dead, what did this all mean? But he was still too feeble to give full force to the mystery.

Holmes then heard muffled speech on the other side of that door. One voice was Curtis. The other sounded like a woman. But Abigail was supposed to be in town; and since

Holmes' strength was still small, he drifted back to sleep wondering.

But he had noticed that the wrist chain given him by the Tsar as a token of thanks was still on his wrist.

When Holmes awoke, his blurred eyes beheld what appeared to be a hermaphroditic, two-headed chimera. But as his eyes cleared and the two heads moved, he saw it was Curtis, and, he guessed, Abby.

"I'm Abby." That confirmed that. "How are you?" Not "ya." Holmes thought to himself.

"Fine, thanks to you. Thank you."

"Oh, that's all right. I had nothing better to do anyway. Do you think you're fit enough to sit up and take some real nourishment?"

As he propped himself up, with the proffered aid of both, Holmes readily agreed, ate heartily, then prepared himself for the American inquisition sure to come.

"Hank tells me you're an Englishman." She laughed as she continued. "We threw you all out over a hundred years ago, and you keep coming back, anyway."
Holmes laughed. "Well, this time I had no choice. But had I known the royal treatment I would receive, I would have gladly washed up on your shores years ago." They all laughed.

"Really, I must repay you all for your kindness to me. I'm not without funds. Once I can correspond with my bank in London, I will repay you for all you've done."

"Hank, this gentleman is obviously still out of his head. He doesn't seem to understand that what we've done is simple American courtesy."

"No, no," Holmes said," I don't wish to offend you nor your courtesy, but this is really too much. I must be able to make this up to you."

"Well, then, James, get well quickly and get out!" She laughed.

"And she means it, Jim. Abby means it."

"I shall do everything within my power to retrieve my health and strength and be
on my way as soon as possible." Then his jovial mood changed radically. "There is much that I must do. There is much that I must do."

At that, Hank and Abby looked at each other and turned to leave Holmes alone once more. That's when Holmes noticed the handle of a revolver Abby had in her basket.

Reilly and Lenin and Trotsky and Stalin

When Reilly left us all in Russia, he said it was at his government's behest; Secret Intelligence Service, to be exact. He was Cheka Colonel Relinsky, and had become so firmly entrenched within the Cheka hierarchy, the Bolsheviks' dreaded secret police, that SIS had instructed him to launch a counter-revolution.

Had it succeeded, with Reilly at the head of a new pro-Western government with strings pulled at Whitehall, perhaps even ready to re-enter the war, the turn in human events could have proved to be nothing short of astounding.

Reilly had become a trusted political pet of Lenin, who referred to him as his bulldog. He had been a huge fan of my accounts of Holmes' and my adventures, which he read when exiled in Switzerland; and he had never forgotten the favor Reilly had done by introducing him to Holmes and me in Petrograd and his boyish joy when we gave him our autographs.

Leon Trotsky, the founder and commander of the Red Army, had an even greater affinity for Reilly. He was wise enough to see how useful Reilly could be. If the Red Army and the Cheka were allied, nothing could stand in the way of Trotsky achieving supreme power.

He had often said, "Not believing in force is the same as not believing in gravity." Wielding the Red Army as your hammer turned everyone else into nails.

However, there was a significant new actor upon that bewildering Bolshevik stage; an important member of the Bolshevik Party's Central Committee, and already a deadly enemy of Trotsky and a malevolent genius of the first order. His name was Iosif Dzhugashvili.

He was a rather small, repugnant Georgian with an already marked ability to remain in the underbrush, sniffing and waiting for the perfect moment to pounce on his prey. A man with no scruples, no morals, no wish for anything other than to make himself the undisputed master of the nascent Soviet Union. He would kill, or have killed, anyone who stood in his way; including Lenin; and, most certainly, Trotsky.

History would come to know this man as Stalin.

Knowing these things about Stalin, Trotksy drew Reilly even closer. He knew that in the inevitable and ultimate confrontation with Stalin, anyone as brilliant and ruthless at obfuscation as Reilly would be an indispensable ally.

In addition, Trotsky already knew Reilly was SIS. With Reilly at his side, perhaps England might be persuaded to come to his aid at his inevitable and crucial clash with Stalin.

The exposing of Reilly's true identity was the doing of the evil head of the Cheka, Felix Dzerzhinsky, also known as "Bloody Felix"; so subtle and serpentine, that he was playing everyone against everyone else without anyone seemingly knowing it.

Dzerzhinsky sniffed the acrid air and decided the wind was blowing in Stalin's direction; so he allied firmly with Stalin.

Reilly was then forced to flee, aided in his escape back to Finland by Trotsky; Trotsky thereby incurring further enmity from Stalin. Stalin, too, would have had use for Reilly. After all, as Stalin said, "Traitors are only traitors if they're not on your side."

What amazed me in his telling of all this, was that Reilly was actually enjoying the memory. He was laughing as he remembered all these titans of history that to him were mere comrades or enemies. Men who either tried to kill him or help him, but in the end, Reilly survived.

At this time, Reilly still did not know that he had become a father; although he was still in love with Tatiana and now, more than ever, wanted to rejoin her. But where?

With papers of safe passage supplied by Trotsky, he was off to find out.

Holmes Leaves For New York

In the space of seven days, Holmes was himself again. Or rather, he was James Hamilton. But whoever he was, he needed to leave as soon as possible and do all that needed to be done. And to have answered all the questions demanding answers.

Hank was kind enough, one morning, to bring his wagon about and drive Holmes the few miles into Port Royal so that he could contact his bank in London and have funds wired to James Hamilton, of course.

To continue the fiction, Holmes said he was notifying Bermuda of his safety, telling them that he would be returning to London and asking to please ship his belongings to his home there.

This was done quickly enough, but while waiting for the transfer, Holmes could not but wonder at the profusion of U.S. Marines and sailors in town.

"Hank, is there a naval base about?"

"Naval base? Bite your tongue, friend. Ain't ya never heard of Parris Island?"

"You mean the United States Marine installation?"

"That's the one, Jim. Yeah, we're still trainin' 'em and sendin' 'em off to help you Brits beat the Krauts. The sailors are just around to row the Marines to Europe and clean up their slop."

At that, Hank's smiling expression changed, and, looking directly into Holmes' eyes, he said, "Ya know, Jim, I suspect there just might be more to you and what happened to you then you're lettin' on."

"I don't understand," Holmes said.

"Well, ya seem like such a smart fella an' all, bein' a fish doctor, that I just can't imagine you gettin' yourself into the predicament you were in when we fished ya outa the water."

"Well, Hank, even scientists can be fools from time to time."

"Yup, I guess you went and proved that." They both laughed.

Presently, Holmes received his funds and he offered compensation to Hank.

"My, oh my, it seems yer memory is still quite on the fizzle", Hank said.

"How do you mean?" asked Holmes.

"Well I seem to remember Abby tellin' ya that what we did was simple courtesy. From one human bein' to another. Or don't they have that in England no more?"

"Yes, of course we do. And it is very much appreciated. But I would like to repay you and your family in some tangible way."

"Well, I'll tell ya what," Hank said as they walked back to the wagon, "once ya get back t' yer institute, or London, just stay there and be safe. We don't wanna be fishin' ya outa the water again."

"A simple request that can be granted with simple alacrity,"   Holmes said.

"If not sooner," Hank said.

Now let's get back to home and you can get the things we gave ya, say goodbye to everybody and get out!" They both laughed again. But Holmes took note once more that

Hank was more than the simple vocabulary-deprived man he appeared to be. He knew the meaning of the word 'alacrity'.

After some hasty stops at local stores for Holmes to purchase a travel valise, some clothing and necessities, and booking passage on a mail carrier due to leave for New York that very afternoon, they went back to the Curtis home.

Holmes gathered the clothes they had given him, packed his new valise with them and the new purchases he'd just made, and went to say goodbye to Abby.

"I can't thank you all enough for what you've done for me."

"Then don't. Just get going to where you're going and don't worry about us, we won't miss you," Abby said.

"And now I suppose I have to bring ya back t' town so ya can get on that ship to New York to take ya back to London. And not a minute too soon, too," Hank said.

Abby gave Holmes a long, warm hug.

"Okay, stop huggin' my wife. Get in so I can get ya to the boat in time."

With that, Holmes and Hank were off to Port Royal again.

It didn't take long to get to the dock where a small ship was being readied to cast off. The *Mercury* was a small mail carrier plying the east coast of the United States. She took parcels as well as passengers, and Holmes was to be one of those passengers.

Hank helped Holmes aboard with his belongings and Holmes reached out his hand to him.

"Once again, Hank, I will never forget you or your family and what you've done for me. And please thank Lou

34

and Martin for their excellent eyesight and strong arms. I wish them well."

Suddenly Hank's speech pattern changed. It seemed that now he wanted to confide in Holmes.

"No worries, Jim. My family and I know you mean what you say. And I trust that you know we never bought that tale you told about how you got where you were. No, Jim, it was better you take us for the simple folk you expected. And as for those young Marines you noted, my oldest son, Don, is over there fighting in France. He was at Bealleau Wood .

"That was one hell of a fight, the papers said. I know you probably didn't hear, but after that battle, the Krauts called the Marines, Tuefel Hunden, Devil Dogs. Not a bad appellation, at that.

"Yes, Don's a Marine and a Curtis, and he came out all right. And by the way, Lou and Martin are back at Parris Island. But they're going to remain Stateside. For now, anyway."

"That's very good to hear, Hank. But just so you know, when I saw a revolver handle in Abby's basket, and your casual understanding of words like alacrity, ichthyologist and Pandora, I suspected there was more there than met the eye, as well. Is there?"

"Well, Jim, let's just say you've got secrets to keep and my family and I may want to keep some secrets, as well."

"Fair enough," Holmes said.

With that, Hank turned and just before he walked across the plank to the deck, he turned, stood ramrod straight, gave a perfect and precise Marines salute to Holmes, said, "Semper Fi, friend, Semper Fi," and walked back to his wagon.

"So," Holmes thought to himself, "much more there, as I suspected. But what?"

On the *Mercury,* Holmes was alone to ponder during the two days it took to get to Manhattan Harbour. His fear for my fate gnawed at him constantly. Once in Manhattan he could, anonymously, learn more of me through an associate in London, but how was he to learn of the fate of Reilly, the Romanovs and the rest? He certainly could not approach those who knew of the secret events because any of them could have been the architect of the assassination attempt. But who? And why?

He would lay the groundwork for his return to London in New York. Then, once returned to London, he would learn of the man, or men, upon whom he would take terrible revenge.

Reilly Finds a Finnish Friend

Hurriedly leaving Petrograd with his papers of safe transport from Trotsky, and wishing to keep ahead of what always seemed to be a brutal Finnish winter, it was early October, 1918, Reilly made his way across the Isthmus of Karelia to Viipuri, on the border of Russia and Finland; only about seventy-five miles from Petrograd and about one hundred and fifty miles from Helsinki.

Today, because of the Russo-Finnish Winter War, Viipuri is known as Vyborg and in Soviet territory. The spoils of a bully.

There, he was able to contact someone who would be able to help him further. They met at a little café, "Pieni Kahvila", which literally translates from Finnish as Little Café.

Yrjö, pronounced "Oor-yuh" - George, in English, was a Finnish double-agent; who, like Reilly, was working for both SIS and the Bolsheviks. However, Yrjö's loyalty,

as it would turn out, was more to honour and to Finland, than to his two seeming masters.

"So, I am to see you safely to Helsinki," Yrjö said as he and Reilly sat down. To Reilly's practiced eye, Yrjö was quite young, in his early twenties; tall, firmly built and as appealing as the birch trees so prevalent throughout Finland. And for someone in their profession, he had an anomalous aura of authentic, innate goodness.

"If it's not too much trouble," Reilly said.

"No trouble, at all, comrade," Yrjö said with a smile. Reilly detected a distinct British accent in Yrjö's speech.

"Oxford?" Reilly asked.

"Very good. Yes. For a time. But please, we're not here to discuss my pitiful personal history, we're here to get you to Helsinki as quickly as possible, then on a ship back to London. If that's all right with you, of course?"

"That suits me perfectly, thank you," Reilly said.

He warmed to Yrjö's sense of humor; but there were many, in the past, who knew when the time was ripe for a joke or a bullet. For some reason, though, Reilly immediately trusted Yrjö. Of course, in his business, that could be a fatal flaw. But not with this man, he felt. Not with this man.

"Here are your papers, Roland," Yrjö said as he took them from inside his jacket pocket.

"Roland?" As Reilly opened the passport, he saw that someone else in SIS had his perverse sense of humor, because he was now Roland Windsor.

"Roland Windsor?" Reilly ruminated, "Yes, indeed; why not?"

As hot black coffee was placed before them, Yrjö said, "Here's to a very safe journey, Roland."

"Here's to a very safe journey, George." They knocked cups, eyes smiled, and sipped slowly.

However, what Reilly and Yrjö did not know, was that they were only a few steps ahead of a secret group called The Patriots, tethered to Stalin. These men, one step above mere murderers, were led by Nicholai Enelkin, a particularly unpleasant butcher; and as cunning as a famished fox.

Enelkin had been trained so thoroughly by Dzerzhinsky, that he could follow a person through the Amazon or the Artic with just a button as a clue. It was Enelkin's job to find Reilly and bring him back. Or if that was not possible, to be sure he would not be going anywhere again; and to eliminate anyone who stood in his way.

Enelkin and three of these Patriots had followed Reilly from Russia through Karelia to Helsinki, always just a bit behind. Enelkin and his men arrived at the café a few minutes after Reilly and Yrjö had left. The waiter pointed to the direction they had gone. To Enelkin, that was a good beginning.

After three days of uneventful travel via train, cart and foot, Reilly and Yrjö reached Helsinki. They had raced, or jolted, depending on the mode of transport, through towns like Hamina, Loviisa, and Porvoo, each sporting the ever-present stands of birch trees and to Reilly's mind, seemingly stoic, unsmiling and unfriendly Finns.

At one point, as if reading Reilly's mind, Yrjö said, "We're not unfriendly, at all, Roland. It just takes us awhile to warm up.

"Here, imagine a frigid Finnish winter; harsh and very uninviting. Then the spring thaw, the blooming of flowers and the welcome warmth of the sun. That's us Finns. Once we thaw out and warm to you, we're the best friends you could have. We'd give you the shirts off our back; especially if we're going to the sauna. Then we'd give up all our clothing." Both laughed.

Yrjö took Reilly to a safe location on Kalevalankatu, Kalevalan Street in English, in a residential district not far from a small harbour and an open-air market on the Gulf of Finland.

Yrjö then went off to book transit for Reilly to London. As it happened, The *Merenneito*, Finnish for "The Mermaid", was due to leave for London the very next day. None too soon for Reilly or Yrjö; because as soon as Reilly was on that ship and off to London, Yrjö could breathe easily again. But he most certainly would not be able to do so until then.

Late that night, as an inordinately hard rain strafed Reilly and Yrjö as they neared their safe location after a fine Finnish restaurant dinner of meat, potatoes and a surfeit of vodka, they didn't notice the two men following, nor the other man who quietly and suddenly appeared in front of them, coming from behind some of the stalls in the darkened market, already closed.

The man in front called out to Reilly in Russian, from a distance of no more than ten feet, "Good evening, Comrade Colonel. Perhaps you might like to come with us and get out of this horrid rain?"

Though Reilly had to keep rubbing his eyes because of the incessant downpour, as did the man in front, he saw the man had a revolver in his hand. Now, hearing the men behind, Yrjö instinctively turned towards them, his back touching Reilly's; and he saw that they, too, had pistols in their hands. The two advancing men stopped; but they held their pistols pointing directly at Yrjö's head.

Reilly answered in Russian, aware that Yrjö understood the conversation, "Oh, come now, comrade. You and your little friends didn't come all this way just for a few nocturnal pleasantries?" As he said this, his right hand moved almost imperceptibly in the rain and dark, until he found his pistol behind his back.

"Thank you for making them angry," Yrjö said, beneath his breath.

The man in front took one step closer. He continued to speak in Russian, "Of course not, comrade. We are here to take you on a little journey, you and your Finnish friend."

"You see, Reilly, even this Russian dog knows that we Finns do make friends," Yrjö said very quietly.

"Well, comrade, my Finnish friend and I are quite exhausted after our last journey, and I truly can't see beginning another one. But I can see you taking one."

With that, Reilly pulled out his pistol with lightning speed and fired, sending the man face downwards into the water-soaked street.

Yrjö then fired instantaneously, felling one man. The other was about to take his shot at Yrjö when Reilly, seeing what was about to happen, pushed Yrjö aside and shot him. However one of the Patriots' bullets connected with Yrjö's right arm. As Yrjö felt the bullet shatter the bone, he fell to one knee.

"I told you not to make them angry," he said.

Reilly saw that while Yrjö was wounded, it was not serious, so he went to the man he shot, as Yrjö did the same to his two targets.

Reilly prodded him with his pistol. He was alive, but badly wounded in his stomach, perhaps fatally.

"There, there, comrade," Reilly said, making sure the man had no more weapons. He held his head in his hands, the rain still raging in torrents.

"Tell me, who are you? Who sent you? If you tell me, I can get a doctor for you and promise that you'll live. If you don't tell me, I can make another promise. You'll die." Reilly placed his pistol against the man's temple. Then he pressed it even more tightly.

"Comrade, comrade, you're a smart man. Surely you want to live," Reilly said.

"Da, da," the man stammered, "I want to live."

"Good, good. So, now tell me, who sent you and who are you?"

"Enelkin, Nickolai Enelkin."

"Good, very good. Now is that your name or the name of the man who sent you?"

The man was spitting up blood now, "My…my name."

"All right, then who sent you?" This time Reilly put the pistol into the man's ear and cocked it.

"Stalin. Stalin. He wants you…back… to question you…to learn things."

"Oh, to learn things, I see. Well, I have something for you to learn; I lied about helping you live." And with that, Reilly pulled the trigger.

"It's good the rain is covering the gunshots," Yrjö said as he came next to Reilly, looking down at Enelkin. Reilly motioned with his head in the direction of the other two. "They, too are taking that journey," Yrjö said, then asked, "Did he give you any information?" He was holding his right arm with his left for support.

"He said Stalin sent him. His name was Enelkin."

"Enelkin? I know that name. He led a special group for Stalin. They did the work too difficult, or distasteful, for others. It's good he's dead. He was not human."

"We have to get out of here and tend to that arm. But first I'm going to drag them over to the harbour and dump them into the Gulf. Will you be all right?"

"Yes; the current should take them far away, especially with the wind and rain," Yrjö said. "It will give our police something more to do than investigate peddlers of rotten fish."

Reilly returned about ten minutes later, and though further drained from the extra exertion, he said, "Here, let me help," as he put his arm around Yrjö to bolster his walking.

"Not needed. We Finns have 'sisu'."

"Oh," said Reilly, not knowing what he meant, making a mental note to ask him later, but not wanting Yrjö to expend any more energy than necessary as they slowly walked back to their haven on Kalevalankatu.

"Reilly, I owe you one."

"Only one? I thought you Finns had nine lives," Reilly joked.

"Only our wives," Yrjö joked back.

What neither noticed because of the dark and rain, was a fourth man. A man who had silently watched and remained hidden.

Holmes Meets "The Brain"

Once in New York and in contact with that associate in London, Holmes was able to set his mind at ease as to my well-being and also that of his brother, Mycroft. But of Reilly, the Romanovs and the rest, his mind still churned. But he was absolutely astonished to learn of his own death and that he was a national war hero.

He knew stories like that are spread throughout the Empire and the world from such heights as blizzards fall. So he began to postulate, and shiver. But if I had been left in peace, perhaps the others had, as well. Then why had he, alone, been a mortal target?

For a little more than a year after arriving in New York, it was now late October, 1919, Holmes examined every possibility, every nuance, every microscopic bit of information that he could extract from his prodigious memory to discover who had been responsible for the attempt on his life; though he, as yet, had not come to a definitive conclusion. As he had so frequently reminded me, "When you have eliminated the impossible, whatever remains, however improbable, must be the truth." This didn't seem to help him now.

His plan was simple, and, based upon subsequent events, so malevolently coincidental, that I believe there were forces of nature at play that I will not even begin to divine. The fear for me, even at this late passage of time, is still palpable. You will learn why, presently.

Holmes' reasoning was thus: he would remain deceased so that he had no fear of any further attempts at assassination. Then, free of that fear, he could begin to lay plans to safely return to London, discover the true identities of those responsible for this death, and wreak his revenge.

But, perhaps, the most disquieting part of his plan was to assume the identity of his complete opposite, John Clay. Yes, John Clay.

Having almost been assassinated at the hands of those who should have been his shield, I don't know if Holmes had become unhinged. He was always fragile, that fine line between genius and madness on which we ruminate.

It had become his firm belief that since he could no longer trust those he thought he could previously trust, he would turn to those who opposed them; strong criminal elements whose affiliations might merge with those of Clay. He was following the dictum, "the enemy of my enemy is my friend."

Of course, he had no idea that Clay was searching for him.

He would find strong allies he absolutely knew had nothing to do with his government's perfidy; allies he may need to call upon for what lay ahead. Quite frankly, allies more ruthless and seemingly unconcerned by their ruthlessness, than anyone in Holmes' memory; the emerging American gangsters.

Since Holmes considered himself to be the intellectual pinnacle of whichever world he chose to inhabit at any particular moment, he would aim for the top man. His circumspect inquiries led him to the man they called "The Brain", "Mr. Big", "The Big Bankroll" and "The Fixer". In fact, the man who had recently fixed the largest sporting event in America, the 1919 World Series, generating the infamous "Black Sox" scandal.

This was the man who controlled much of the burgeoning underworld; especially illegal gambling. This was the man who Holmes learned was a distant business associate of Clay's, but who had never met him personally. Indeed, he was the man who Holmes regarded as the American Clay. This was the man who Holmes chose to become his ally.

His name was Arnold Rothstein.

Holmes learned that because of the coming of Prohibition in America, of which I will speak more of later in in this narrative, Rothstein and Clay had been formulating a deal for his Scottish distilleries to supply spirits to Rothstein.

Holmes grudgingly admired their international business influence. He thought it would have been sporting to thwart them had not his "death" forced him in a decidedly divergent direction.

Holmes believed no one in New York knew what Clay looked like so he would impersonate Clay to the hilt; and though some may have known of Holmes, a simple disguise would solve that problem. It had to be real, though, so he grew a mustache, full beard and colored all his hair a cross between russet and brown.

But as Reilly relayed, it was more than a disguise, for when they met for the first time, Holmes seemed to have changed physically. Not just with age, but his whole persona seemed to have darkened. Those were Reilly's words precisely, "His whole persona seemed to have darkened." Chilling words. Chilling.

From what Reilly recounted further, Holmes, though further on in age, had now become enmeshed in the social and literary nightlife of New York. As Clay, a supposed master British criminal with a rapier intellect, he lent an air of danger to pampered literati and feted Broadway celebrities.

Of course he would do nothing to overtly draw attention from the authorities, but it was his belief that any new acquaintance made at this level of public fascination, might be of future help in his overarching search for retribution.

He became a regular of Manhattan's famed Algonquin Roundtable and could be seen in battles of verbal barbs with the intellectually glittering likes of Alexander Woollcott, George S. Kaufman, Robert Benchley and Dorothy Parker. They called themselves "The Vicious Circle" and all would defer to Holmes for a mortal, terminating retort.

Yet it was not only these titans of the literary set who would attend the festivities. Holmes struck up friendships with the great American baseball behemoth Babe Ruth, the legendary thespian Tallulah Bankhead, and the World's

Heavyweight Boxing Champion, Jack Dempsey. To all, Holmes was Clay. And to Holmes, all were pieces of a puzzle that were to fall into a particular place when needed.

Holmes gleefully reported tweaking Ruth's nose, only to find that Ruth "hit one out of the park" at him:

"Mr. Ruth, I understand that you are the king of your sport; something akin to cricket."

"Hey, 'keed'," to Ruth everyone was 'keed', "I swing a bat, not bugs."

That garnered an incredible laugh from all around the table, not the least of whom was Holmes who rarely was bested verbally or otherwise.

Holmes spoke of Dempsey and he playfully jabbing at each other while members of The Vicious Circle, and joyful onlookers, rooted uproariously for one or the other to connect with a decisive punch. After all, Holmes reminded Reilly, he had been a singular amateur boxer in his youth.

Above all, there was the American underworld. The men who were part of that sinister brotherhood were already organizing to take advantage of the passage of the Eighteenth Amendment to the American Constitution, better known as Prohibition.

This bizarre law which would ban the creation, sale and distribution of alcoholic beverages had been ratified by the American congress on January 16, 1919. It was to go into formal effect quite soon, on January 17, 1920.

Through particular intermediaries, pieces of the puzzle now used, a meeting was set with Holmes to meet Rothstein at his office suite at Manhattan's Park Central Hotel, on Seventh Avenue and 55th Street, slightly north of the Great White Way.

What happened at that meeting harkens back to my previous mention of a malevolent coincidence.

As Holmes approached the Park Central Hotel, he noticed three young men by the entranceway. By their dress, these men were not hotel employees. They wore camel-hair or mohair overcoats against the November chill. Their wide-brimmed fedoras were expensive and color-matched to their overcoats. Holmes noticed razor-creases in the trousers showing below the elongated overcoats and exquisitely polished lizard-clad shoes below the trousers.

Holmes wondered how three such young men would have the funds to expend on such finery. His answer came swiftly.

The men noticed this stranger approaching and, in unison, turned towards Holmes, all thrusting their hands into their overcoats, and taking one step towards him. But one took two.

"Who you?" Curt question asked, this man's hand stayed firmly in his overcoat and his body rocked to-and-fro ominously towards Holmes; as would a king cobra in front of its charmer.

This man was the youngest of the group, looking no more than in his late teens, muscular and tall. But it was his ice-blue eyes that truly caught Holmes' attention. They were, perhaps, the eyes of a nascent psychopath. They were held menacingly wide open and even without the "Who you?" were demanding an answer.

"My name is John Clay. I have an appointment with Mr. Rothstein at ten."

"Ya talk funny, Johnny. Where ya from, Philly?"

"Why, no, London."

"Ya mean like in England?"

"Yes, as in England."

With his head tilted slightly backward towards the other men, "Hey, we got a guy here from England. He says he got an appointment with Mr. Rothstein." The men said nothing and stood with their hands as before, inside their overcoats and apparently clutching pistols.

"You know the King?" this man asked.

"No, we've never met," Holmes answered.

"Well, I ain't met the president, neither, so I guess we're even. Here, lift yer arms, I gotta frisk ya." With that, Holmes raised his arms, the young man patted him from armpit to foot, then stood upright again.

"He's clean," he said to the men in back, with that same head-tilt, never taking those iceberg eyes off Holmes.

"Let him by. Mr. Rothstein is expecting him, remember?" This came from the man in the longest camel-hair overcoat. The one Holmes now knew to be the leader of this curious Yankee troika. And he now knew from where these young men drew their funds.

"Oh, yeah," said ice-eyes. "Damn, Johnny boy, I thought I could dust ya, now I gotta make nice to ya. Screwy world, huh?"

"Yes, quite."

"Ya still talk funny."

"Here, come up here". The long camel hair overcoat gestured Holmes to follow him. The third man followed in back of Holmes. This man was quite short, only about five-foot-four, but when Holmes had a quick look at his face, he saw steel.

As Holmes followed the leader, ice-eyes called out, "Yeah, and give my love to the King and Queen if you see 'em, okay?"

"Of course."

The leader took the group through the hotel lobby, nothing fancy, then to the elevator. As they walked, Holmes noticed the way in which others in the lobby would part to facilitate the trio's progress.

"Mr. Rothstein told me you'd be here. We're goin' up to his suite. You just follow me and Meyer will just follow you. Benny's staying down here."

"Of course. Whatever procedure might be best."

"Yeah." This man looked to be in his mid-twenties, but carried himself as the leader he already knew he was. The short one, the one now in back of Holmes, looked to be a bit younger.

As they got into the elevator, they both faced Holmes and he was able to finally a good luck at both of the men, who had now doffed their fedoras.

The leader was about five-foot-ten, lean, with a hard, pock-marked face and wavy black hair. His dark eyes stared straight at Holmes with neither menace nor contempt, nor with any discernable expression, for that matter. Holmes realized that to this man, he was nothing. Just a parcel to be delivered, un-damaged, to his master, Arnold Rothstein.

The small man was a different story. His eyes kept studying Homes from head to toe and back again, never stopping in the few scant minutes it took to arrive on the ninth floor, where Rothstein had his suite. But to Holmes, those few minutes told insightful tales.

When the elevator doors opened, they turned right and right again around a corner and there Holmes saw another young man, also in his twenties, about the same height as the leader, a bit corpulent, and with a rather nasty scar along the left side of his face. He noticed us and became rigid.

"Relax, Al. This guy's here to see Mr. Rothstein."

"Okay." He opened the door but stayed outside as Holmes and his two escorts went in.

They all stood in the middle of what appeared to be a sparse foyer. Then the only door leading further inside opened. Arnold Rothstein walked out. He was of medium height, slight of build, slicked back black hair, much younger than Holmes had imagined, in this late thirties, and dressed in what Americans might consider a gentleman's attire; an artfully tailored suit, complete with waistcoat.

"Mr. Rothstein, Benny said this guy's here to see you."

"Mr. Rothstein," Holmes said.

"Mr. Clay. Please come in. It's nice to finally meet you after our transatlantic courtship. I hope we can make this 'shittach' happen."

"Pardon me?"

"Sorry, John, That was Yiddish for 'marriage'. Sometimes I forget that not everyone speaks Yiddish."

Though Rothstein was being charming, Holmes was well aware of Rothstein's nefarious acumen, and now, able to look into Rothstein's eyes, he was finally able to gauge the wheels upon wheels and tumbling gears behind them. Perhaps Rothstein was more calculator than corporeal being.

"Please call me Arnold," Rothstein said.

"Very well, then, Arnold."

A big smile crossed Rothstein's face, as if he had just completed his first move of successful seduction.

"So I guess I can call you John?"

"I don't surmise it would hurt."

Another smile from Rothstein.

As Holmes followed Rothstein into his office, he was surprised at the minimum of extrannea; essentials and nothing more. Which mirrored Rothstein, himself.

"So, John, what's on your mind? What do we have to do to shake hands?"

"I believe you're already aware of that. Someone with your intellect, interest and incisive disposition has already decided that this meeting would, indeed, bring our hoped-for endeavor to a mutually beneficial conclusion or there would have been no meeting."

Rothstein laughed again. Louder, this time, with an inflection intimating his appreciation of the kindred intelligence of the man before him.

"Right-O, John. You hit the nail on the head. You have the distilleries in Scotland and I have a whole damn country filled with yokels who want to drink the stuff. You have supply, I have demand, we have a deal?" He extended his hand.

Now it was Holmes' turn to laugh. Not only at the presumption of Rothstein but at his witty encapsulation of the state of the United States.

"I've appreciate how quickly you Americans come to the point, but, I believe, you may be putting the cart before the horse?"

"How come?" His hand was withdrawn with a slight frown.

"Well before one can agree on a deal, one must have a clear appreciation of what, precisely, that deal might be."

That laugh again.

"Yeah, yeah,'course, 'course. You were supposed to come up with a price per crate of the scotch, delivered by your ships offshore to where I tell you and if it sounded good, we shake hands, have a drink on it and we have a deal."

"And if we cannot agree on a price?"

At this, his facial disposition hardened.

"Well then, John, if you're not selling to me, you might decide to sell to one my, shall we say 'competitors', and that just wouldn't do."

"Oh, I see."

"I certainly hope so."

The presumption, once again, on Rothstein's part, that the hint of a threat might unnerve him, gave Holmes further insight into Rothstein's egomania or complete and matter-of-fact acceptance of his power.

"John, you met some of my boys outside."

"Oh, yes, interesting young men."

"Well, those interesting young men are more interesting than you could know. Let me clue you in.

"Charlie Luciano, the one you can spot as the leader of those guys, is a Sicilian, but he thinks like us.

"Benny Siegel, the guy you left in front of the hotel, may be just a kid, but he's already killed three guys. That we know of.

"And Meyer Lansky, the little man. Imagine me at his age and that's Meyer. Yeah, he's short, but let me tell ya, he and Benny were runnin' a real tough gang before they came to work for me. It was called 'the Bugs and Meyer Mob'."

"Bugs?" Holmes asked.

"Yeah. Benny is a little, shall we say, nuts. So some guys started in calling him Bugsy, a nickname. He didn't like it. They didn't call him that anymore. So never, ever, call him Bugsy. His name is Ben or Benny or Benjamin; but never Bugsy."

"Thank you. Benjamin will suit. As in Disraeli."

Rothstein continued. "Disraeli. Very good. And that's just the tip. I got guys all over the country. I got that kid outside the door, from Brooklyn, Al Capone, going up to Chicago to work for a friend of mine, Johnny Torrio. Johnny runs Chicago. Like Browning said: 'Ah, but a man's reach should exceed his grasp, or what's a heaven for?' Right?"

"In that case..." But before Holmes could speak, Rothstein cut him short. He was tiring of his cat and mouse.

"Nah, don't waste your time. The game has gone on long enough. John Clay, I very much would like you to meet someone."

"And whom might that be?" asked Holmes.

"John Clay."

Reilly Leaves For London

After tending to Yrjö's wound and satisfied there would be no lasting ill effect, Reilly and Yrjö finally fell into a fitful sleep.

There would be no more intrusion to mar that night, nor any the next day as Reilly was ready to board The *Merenneito*.

"Well, my Finnish friend, we seemed to have had a bit of an adventure."

"My arm says so," Yrjö said. "But, Roland, you are now on your own. I won't be there to take any more bullets for you."

"Now that's a comforting thought."

"I wish you luck with what you must do, and to find the peace you deserve once you have done it," Yrjö said.

"That's practically poetic," Reilly said.

"I guess you never read *Kalevala*." Yrjö said.

"Yrjö, before I leave, I want to ask a question. Personal courtesy. Do you know who I am?"

"Personal courtesy?" Yrjö made a show of rubbing his chin as one does when in deep thought. "Roland, we have no such thing as personal courtesy in what we do."

Reilly shrugged, and after a gentle handshake so as not to disturb Yrjö's wounded arm, he went up onto the deck. He turned to see Yrjö with a very broad smile and waving slowly, with his good arm, of course.

"You see, Sidney, what good friends we Finns can be?" he shouted as *Merenneito* carefully left the dock.

So Yrjö knew his name, after all. Of course, he'd know.

"I do know now, I most certainly do," Reilly shouted back. And in short order, the ship pulled out of Yrjö's sight.

Also out of sight of both Yrjö and Reilly, hidden from view, near the far right bow, stood the man who stood hidden in the dark and the rain the night before.

Mr. Clay, I Presume

Another door opened, towards the right in Rothstein's office and through it walked John Clay. A very startled John Clay.

"Holmes!"

"Clay."

Clay went quickly to Holmes and began shaking his hand, which, of course, completely startled Holmes, not knowing that Clay had come to America in search of him.

As Holmes fought to gain composure, Clay said, "Well, I should think the least I should expect from you is something akin to 'What on earth are you doing here?', or some such drollery."

Rothstein watched the two men as a Roman emperor had watched two gladiators in the ring. Clay noticed Rothstein's Cheshire-cat-grin and decided to show this American that perhaps he was not as omniscient as he thought. He looked at Rothstein and said, "Mr. Arnold Rothstein, I have the rapturous pleasure of presenting to you, Mr. Sherlock Holmes."

Clay received the reaction he had hoped from Rothstein; total and complete incredulity.

"Holmes? The limey dick?"

Holmes gave Rothstein a raised eyebrow.

"Oh, come, come, Arnold; surely you mean the great British consulting detective," said Clay, taking deep delight in Rothstein's continued discomfort. "Arnold, say 'hello' to Mr. Holmes; he's really a quite interesting fellow."

Rothstein was angry. "You think this is funny, Clay? You think this is one big joke?" His voice was so loud now that Luciano and Lansky came running in with pistols drawn.

Rothstein waved them away. "Nah, nah, put the gats down, boys, but keep 'em ready. These two Brits just tried to put one over on me, but it didn't work."

It was Lansky who spoke. "We know who this guy is, Mr. Rothstein," nodding his head towards Holmes, believing him to be Clay, "but who's that guy?" He was pointing at Clay.

"Not important now. But hang around outside while they explain to me just what the hell is so funny and what the hell is going on."

He turned back to Holmes and Clay once Lansky and Luciano had left the room and closed the door. "Okay, talk. And I don't care which of you opens his trap first." Clay did.

"It's quite simple, really. Arnold, you and I have done business for quite some time through trans-Atlantic cables and trusted intermediaries, but we'd never met. With Prohibition rapidly approaching and our cables about supplying scotch to you and your friends, I thought the time quite ripe for us to finally meet, raise a glass or two, and consummate our arrangement."

"Yeah. so? So what the hell is this Holmes guy doing going around town telling people he's you?" Rothstein asked.

Then he turned to Holmes. "You may be some wise guy dick in London, but I run this town and when somebody goes around saying they're somebody I do business with, but who ain't, I know somethin's screwy. Get me?"

"I can't shed any light on that," Clay said, "but I'm sure Mr. Holmes can." Both Clay and Rothstein were looking at Holmes.

"Yes, well, it's rather elementary, really. But Arnold, before I explain my charade, would it be possible for me to speak with Mr. Clay alone for a brief moment?"

"Why, so you can cook up another scheme?" asked Rothstein.

"No, no scheme, I can assure you. But there are certain matters I need to discuss with Mr. Clay which would impact any arrangement the two of you might conclude; and I promise, Arnold, this will only be to your ultimate benefit."

Clay looked at him suspiciously, but was shrewd enough to know whatever Holmes had in mind would ultimately benefit only Holmes. However, since he was still coming to grips with the fact that this was actually a living, breathing Sherlock Holmes and that his quest to find him was over, he said nothing and nodded assent to Rothstein.

"Okay, okay. Two minutes. But when I come back, you better have some nice big news for me with big green dollars in the headline. Get me?"

"Oh, most assuredly," said Holmes. Clay nodded again in assent.

"I'll leave you two lovebirds alone for two minutes. Then Meyer and Charlie and me'll be back." And with that, he walked out of the room.

"Holmes, you have no idea how happy I am to see you."

Holmes could see, but could not believe, that Clay seemed utterly sincere. "Clay, I have no idea what you mean."

With that, Clay began to divulge what had happened since Holmes had disappeared. Holmes' seeming death at the hands of the Germans, Watson's safe and happy return, and Clay's own quest and promise to Watson to find Holmes.

"As I told Watson, without someone of your caliber to joust with, much of the fun of my crimes was slipping away. I needed my wits constantly sharpened and only your wits served as sharpener."

At first, Holmes maintained his suspicion of Clay, but as he slowly came to believe him and was about to inquire further about what he had learned about his death in London, he and Clay heard shots in the other room. Their first reaction was to stoop for cover, but then, in unison, both bolted for the door.

There, on the floor, lay Rothstein, wounded and bleeding profusely. Luciano and Lansky had already run after those who had fired the shots, but leaving one of them dead already.

Just as Holmes bent down to tend to Rothstein, another gunman suddenly appeared at the doorway and took a shot at the prone body of Rothstein. It would have surely hit Holmes had not Clay dropped in front of Holmes. The bullet hit Clay.

Holmes examined Clay, trying to determine where he had been wounded,

"Why did you do that, Clay?" asked Holmes.

"Ponder it." He gave a faint laugh-cough. "Funny, now you truly must be me," Clay whispered. And with that, the remaining air in lungs slowly slid out and he died.

Luciano and Lansky came running back into the room to see the dead gunman, the dead Clay, the now-dead Rothstein, but a much alive Holmes.

Lansky knelt by Rothstein. "I shoulda protected him better. I shoulda shot those guys first."

Luciano just stood there, pistol still in hand, giving a rational, cold-blooded summation, "Nah, we just got surprised, that's all. It happens. Now what Mr. Rothstein had, maybe we can have. We gotta talk about this with Benny and Al. And you," he was gesturing with his pistol towards Holmes, "we gotta talk to you, too. About the booze. But not now.

"Now we gotta get outta here. The cops'll take care of the bodies. Al got winged at the door, he's downstairs with Benny. Meyer, you go down there with Clay here," he was nodding towards Holmes, "and you," still looking at Holmes, "you go with Meyer to Benny and Al downstairs. You mean too much dough to us now for anything to happen to you, too."

It was obvious to Holmes that Luciano and Lansky believed him to be Clay, since Rothstein had accepted him as such in front of them. Therefore, with Luciano as the new leader, all of Rothstein's underlings would accept him as Clay.

This made it now even more imperative that his original plan move forward. It struck him as cosmically ironic that he, Sherlock Holmes, would have to subsume his identity and henceforth become John Clay, in reality. Then, upon his return to England, with Clay's rule of the London underworld now his, how much easier and vicious would be his vendetta?

Safely escorted by Lansky away from the bloody scene and down to the entrance of the hotel, Holmes was virtually pushed into a mammoth Packard, an American automobile so large that he felt a Rolls Royce could fit comfortably within its interior. Already inside were Siegel at the wheel and Capone in the passenger seat, who, though wounded, turned to Holmes, motioned nonchalantly with his thumb to his face and said, "I had worse."

"We gotta get 'em. We gotta kill 'em all," Siegel was yelling.

"We will," Lansky said, but keep yer mind on yer drivin', Benny."

"Just who is 'them'?" Holmes asked.

"Numbers Malone and his gang," Lansky said. "Damn micks."

"Another example of the American love of apropos nicknames," thought Holmes.

"That Numbers is completely nuts," Siegel yelled. Holmes just listened. "They been comin' down from the Bronx, shakin' down our guys at our joints, wantin' more of the numbers, wantin' more of this, wantin' more of that. I'll give 'em more of my gun in their heads."

"Calm down, Benny. I don't wanna be in no traffic accident," Lansky said.

Siegel drove them to a toney area of Manhattan known as Central Park West, and, as its name implied, bordered the extreme western part of Central Park. They stopped in front of a tall, new Art Deco residential building at 72 Central Park West.

"This is Al's place," said Lansky to Holmes. "Get out." This they all did. Capone in some discomfort. The doorman took the car.

Holmes noted that the entranceway, or lobby, to this building was quite opulent and that not many would be able to afford such luxury. From there, they took the lift to the penthouse. Lansky knocked and the door was opened by someone who appeared to be a cohort of these men, rather than a domestic. Holmes was greeted by even more luxury and a commanding view of Central Park and, it seemed, the entirety of Manhattan.

"Sit," said Lansky, which Holmes proceeded to do, while the men went to a bathroom to tend to dress Capone's wound. All except for Lansky, who sat down opposite Holmes and continued his study of Holmes as assiduously as Holmes studied Lansky.

This Lansky, whose eyes and behavior betrayed an intelligence that eerily reminded Holmes of his own, was the one man of all these men who would never be arrested for anything major and who would, with Charlie Luciano, become the true "inventors", if that is the proper word for anything so improper, of organized crime in America.

"He'll live, the schmuck," Siegel said as he came back and, to use an American colloquialism, plopped himself into a chair next to Lansky. "Dago putz," joked Siegel about Capone.

Benjamin Siegel, with a menacing, misdirected kinetic energy, better known to history as "Bugsy" Siegel, was a true seductive sociopath who could smile and kill with simultaneous ease.

The "Al" to whom he was referring, was Al Capone, a man who, I surmise, needs no detailed introduction. He emerged from the bathroom shortly, arm bandaged, hanging out of his sleeve and held with a makeshift sling of silk.

"I'm definitely gonna go out to Chicago, like Mr. Rothstein wanted," Capone said, lifting his arm and puffing his cheeks in a gesture of "I don't need this grief anymore.

"But first, we get Malone and his guys. I ain't goin' nowhere till they're so dead even rats won't eat 'em."

"Watch yourself, Al," Siegel warned, "I hear Chicago is a very scary town. You can get real hurt in Chicago."

"Very funny, very funny," said Capone, swatting at Siegel's head with his good arm. He and Siegel laughed. Lansky was still looking at Holmes.

Presently, Luciano returned. I should introduce him properly. This was, at the moment, the man known to the New York constabulary as Salvatore Lucania; though he was Charlie Luciano. But within a short space of time, he would be known to the world as "Lucky" Luciano. As previously stated, the man, who, along with Lansky, organized crime in America. But more of that later.

"Hey, Mr. Clay, who the hell was that other guy; none of us saw him go up to Mr. Rothstein?" Luciano asked.

"His name was Glover. He and I were having a business disagreement when Mr. Rothstein intervened. He won't be missed and I removed any identification before we left."

"Smart," Luciano said, admiringly. He sat next to Lansky.

"Maybe he was Houdini and he just appeared in that room. Houdini is Jewish, ya know," Siegel said to Holmes.

"No, I wasn't aware."

"Yeah, his real name is Erich Weiss. Somethin', huh?"

"Most assuredly," agreed Holmes, hoping that Siegel would stop.

Luciano interrupted and Siegel stopped.

"Okay, forget that crap. We should be takin' over from Mr. Rothstein, not Malone and his mob. All the stuff that was Mr. Rothstein's, is now ours." He made a sweeping, circular gesture with his outstretched arms, indicating all the men in the room.

"I'll go up there myself and kill 'em all," Siegel said.

"I appreciate you volunteerin', Ben, but it's gonna take some plannin'," Luciano said.

It was now Holmes turn to interrupt and surprised himself at what he now said.

"Gentlemen, you cannot wait and plan. Right now, this Numbers Malone and his men are up in that Bronx place, probably laughing and drinking and congratulating themselves on killing Mr. Rothstein.

"He probably thinks that you're too young and too disorganized to seek immediate retribution."

"Huh?" Siegel asked.

"Clay is sayin' we go up to the Bronx and take care of 'em now," said Lansky.

"Yes, in any successful military operation, surprise is always a key element. If you wait any longer, they'll just come back down and pick you all off one by one.

"He's right," Capone said.

"I agree," Lansky said.

"So what you're sayin' is that we get some more of our guys and go up there now and end this right away?" Luciano stated, more than asked.

"Precisely," Holmes answered.

Seeing that he was not only being accepted into this unfortunate fold, but had just become an architect of a major crime, he called upon what he knew to be the surface loyalty of felons and took the next step in their business relationship.

"Gentlemen, before we settle the details of how best to eliminate Mr. Malone and his minions, and while this might not be the most propitious of times, would it be improper to conclude the agreement Mr. Rothstein and I were finalizing?" Holmes asked.

"Nah, it's okay," explained Lansky, "Mr. Rothstein was the smartest of the smart. And he could always choose a winner. If he chose you, he already played it from every angle. So you and Charlie and me'll fill in the details later."

"Yeah, first we fill Malone with bullets," Siegel said. Lansky just shrugged.

What would happen over the next few months, while setting Holmes' timetable for retribution behind, in the long run, would only strengthen his ties to these hoodlums and permit him to inflict his very particular brand of retribution on those who had tried to kill him.

Reilly In London, August 2, 1919

Reilly's boat trip to London was happily uneventful; a short respite used to reflect, to suppose and to hope.

Without stopping to report to SIS that he was there, or alive, and to be debriefed, he first came to me. He knew that Yrjö would have alerted London as to his whereabouts.

It was early on the evening of August 2, 1919, when he knocked on my door. He heard me addressing Elizabeth, "Don't mind, Elizabeth, I'll tend to this."

Pause for a moment and, if possible, picture from my point of view, opening the door to find Reilly standing before you. Exactly.

"Wha...wha...Rei..," all I could do was stammer.

Reilly let out a laugh, grabbed me in an all-encompassing bear hug, and stood there silently rocking us for a brief moment.

When he freed me he asked, "Well, am I not to be invited in?"

"Why...why... of course," I was still stammering as if I had just seen the spirit of Christmas past. And in a way, I had.

"Reilly, Reilly, please, in there, in there," I said pointing Reilly to my study. "How, Reilly, how? Pray, tell me everything, I'm so speechless at your sudden appearance."

"Under the circumstances, quite understandable. Watson, might you have a libation to offer a poor traveler?"

"Most assuredly, most assuredly," and I gingerly removed a bottle of aged scotch and two glasses from my desk.

"Ah, that's good scotch, Watson. You're more discerning that I had imagined."

Playing the wounded individual, "Why, Reilly, in all the time we spent together and with your supreme level of intelligence, I am abashed to learn of your failure to discern that." We laughed.

"But, please, Reilly, you left us in July of last year. I cannot even begin to think of the correct questions to ask and in what order."

"No, Watson, wait. Before I tell you, I have one all-important question."

"Yes, yes, of course. But I believe I know what it is. Tatiana is well, at least I believe so. As are all the Romanovs."

Reilly must have let out all the air in his lungs with relief. "Thank heaven for that."

"But, Reilly, there is more. Are you seated securely?"

"Pardon me?"

"Reilly, it gives me the greatest of pleasure to report to you, that you are a father."

For perhaps the first time in his life, Reilly was speechless. And, it seemed, paralyzed, as well.

"It is a boy, Reilly, a boy. He was born on March 2. He is now six months old. And Tatiana named him after you. His name is Sidney."

With that, again perhaps for the first time in his life, Reilly lowered his head and wept.

Holmes Becomes Consigliere

Luciano, Lansky, Siegel and Capone were in one car. Other men with interesting nicknames were in a second: Legs Diamond, Dutch Schultz, Kid Twist Reles and Lepke Buchalter. This last man would go on to found "Murder, Inc."; literally contract killers with no allegiance to anyone or any group.

"It's good we're gonna get those guys now. By tomorrow, we'll have to attend Mr. Rothstein's funeral, if they let him be buried like he's supposed to be," Lansky said. "Ain't no use in any of us stayin' away as the cops know we all worked for him."

All in the first car agreed.

It was early afternoon when the cars pulled up in front of Rusty's, a bar on West Farms Square in the Bronx that was Malone's headquarters. It flourished because it sat on a terminus of trolley cars, buses, an American equivalent to our underground called a subway, and only a few minute walk to one of the world's truly great nature attractions, the Bronx Zoo. The lithe Bronx River ran along the exterior rear of Rusty's.

The men in both cars had either pistols or "Tommy Guns"; so called because they were Thompson submachine guns from WWI. Neither car had any tags or plates of identification.

As Holmes had predicted, Malone and his men were inside drinking, celebrating their killing of Rothstein. They were sloppy and left no guards on the outside.

With almost military precision, all doors swung open and the men from both cars ran into Rusty's. Malone, his seven men and the bartender were completely surprised and held their hands up in surrender.

"Now nobody is gonnna do nothin' stupid," Luciano said. "Guns out, barrel first, and throw 'em on the floor! Now!"

When one of the men looked as if he was going to do something stupid, Siegel shot him in the head and said, "See what happens when you do something stupid?"

Schultz, Diamond and Reles waved all the men except Malone to the far end of the long, oak bar and stood there with their Tommy Guns on the remaining six, including the bartender. Malone remained at mid-bar. Buchalter remained at the front doors, watching.

Luciano walked slowly over to Malone with Siegel, Lansky and Capone right behind.

Malone was the same age and height and had the same ferocity as Luciano, but he didn't have one tenth the brains. Luciano could see the fear in Malone. But Malone didn't think he was showing it.

"So whaddaya gonna do now, Charlie? That Jew ya worked for is dead. Why not join up with me and the guys and we can own this town?" Malone asked.

"I'm Jewish, too," yelled Siegel and he shot Malone in the knee. Malone crumpled. His men made a slight move but Schultz, Diamond and Reles just waved their Tommy Guns and the men moved back.

As Malone lay on the floor howling in pain, Capone kicked him in the wound and said, "We ain't even yet."

Luciano then walked over to the men at the end of the bar.

"T' hell with ya, ya dago piece of garbage," said one of the men.

"See what I mean about doin' stupid' stuff. Now, how the hell stupid do ya have t' be t'curse me out with me and my guys havin' guns on ya and you got your brains up your ass?" Luciano asked.

Capone had come over. "Dago piece a crap, did ya say?" Capone shot him in the testicles. The other men recoiled and grabbed their own in reflex. Capone then gave a nod of the head to Schultz, Diamond and Reles who, with their Tommy Guns, dispatched the other men quickly, professionally, and with no wasted bullets. Diamond stood far enough back so that no blood would spatter his spats. He was unsuccessful.

This left only Malone, still on the floor and still howling in pain.

"Oh gee whiz, Numbers; you're bleedin' all over the nice floor and screechin' like one of your freakin' banshees. You'll wake up the whole damn neighbourhood.

"I know, you need to cool off. How about I take ya for a swim? Would you like that, Numbers?"

With that, Siegel dragged Malone by the neck of his jacket to the back of Rusty's, opened the back door and then dragged Malone down the rocky, little hill to the Bronx River.

"See,Numbers? You're gonna cool off. Forever."

Siegel turned Malone upside down so his head was in the water and he held his head down until Malone had, indeed, cooled off forever.

Siegel then joined the others and they went back to Manhattan.

In Capone's apartment, Holmes had no idea of the savagery he had unwittingly unleashed. He would learn more, however, with time and become more inurned to it; drifting farther into a persona from which it might be impossible to disengage.

Upon their return, Luciano, Lansky and Siegel began to formalize their new partnership with Holmes; Capone would be leaving for Chicago in a few days and whatever his three colleagues decided was fine with him. He knew he'd get what he was due.

"Hey, Meyer, count good," Capone said as a fond goodbye when he finally left for Chicago.

With Capone gone and many of his men with him, Luciano, Lansky and Siegel had to come to grips with the power vacuum left by Rothstein's death; and if not handled properly, would most certainly lead to their own. There were much larger fish than Numbers Malone befouling the filthy waters of the Hudson and the East River.

Salvatore Maranzano and Giuseppe Masseria were the biggest of these fish. While these names remain unknown to most outside of the United States, to New Yorkers of this period, the names literally were equated with evil and death.

With Rothstein gone, the old "Mustache Petes", as they were referred to by Luciano and other young gangsters on the rise, would soon begin a war to divide Rothstein's territory and to enlist his young mobsters into their ranks.

After all, they reasoned, more territory needed more soldiers to protect it. Then you needed more soldiers to conquer more territory and to hold that territory. Ad nauseum. The Roman emperors had taught these men too well.

It was called the Castellammarese War because both Masseria and Maranzano
had emigrated from that region in Sicily. And it was fought brutally and with no quarter. Right on the streets of New York.

Luciano, Lansky and Sigel, though very smart and very tough, did not have the numbers to overtly challenge either Maranzano or Masseria; even with Diamond, Schultz Buchalter and Reles. So they began to quietly gather other young mobsters who wanted no part of the Mustache Petes and who would gladly ally to eliminate Masseria and Maranzano.

The young Sicilian immigrants who fell in with Luciano would all to go on to criminal infamy: Carlo Gambino, Albert Anastasia, Frank Costello, Vito Genovese, and Joe Adonis, to name a few.

Yet in the midst of the war, Holmes continued the planning with his new business partners and tried not to become directly involved.

It was at an intense planning session between Luciano, Lansky, Siegel and Holmes, on how the spirits were to be delivered from Scotland to America that Lansky suddenly changed the topic.

Lansky said, "John, over the last few months, getting to know you and see how you think, and how you helped us with Malone, we agree that you think like Mr. Rothstein and not too many people could do that." Luciano and Siegel nodded assent.

Luciano spoke next. "What Meyer is saying, is that with what we have going on, and which could hurt our business arrangement with you, we want you to be our consigliere."

"I beg your pardon," Holmes said.

Siegel said, "You know, our counselor. Like Meyer said, you got brains. You're like Mr. Rothstein was, may he rest in peace."

Lansky continued, "We need someone to trust as we go to war with them guys. Someone we can plan strategy with and bounce ideas off of, if you know what I mean."

"A consigliere is a very special person in our thing. He's the one who can see all the angles and help us play the right one," Luciano said.

"I see," said Holmes. And knowing that he could not refuse such an important request without fear of suspicion and then, perhaps, worse, he said, "Gentlemen, I am truly honoured that you hold me in such high regard and I solemnly accept your offer."

"Good, it's settled," Luciano said and all three men rose from the table to shake hands with Holmes.

"Imagine that, a limey consigliere. It's like a Hebe Pope," said Siegel.

"Crude, but true. Welcome," Meyer said.

"C'ent anni," Luciano said. "To a hundred years, John."

"Yeah, right. We should live so long," said Siegel.

And with what was to happen to Luciano in the midst of the Castellammarese War, that statement proved preternaturally prescient.

Reilly Leaves London

After Reilly had regained his composure, and with assistance of some brandy, he looked at me and said, "A son. I never imagined that I'd be a father. Not with my life. Never. And tell me again, Tatiana, she's completely all right?"

"Yes, yes. As a doctor and as a friend, when I left her and the family she was fine."

"My God, where are they? Are they in London? Where are they?" He was practically shaking me.

"Calm down, Reilly, calm down. No, they're not here. They're in the Bahamas. On the island of Eleuthera."

"I haven't heard of it."

"Don't worry, it's a beautiful place. I was with them for about a year. And, I must tell you, I'm the one you have to thank for spanking your namesake into the world."

"You, you were the doctor for Tatiana?"

"Well, of course. Who the dickens did you think? The bloody head of the Royal Medical Society?"

"No, no, I meant that I couldn't be happier that Tatiana and the baby were in your hands. They couldn't have been safer."

"Quite true, quite true. Now compose yourself further because Elizabeth will most certainly be here shortly to see just what has become of me. I'll simply introduce you as an old and dear friend from the army, a comrade I haven't seen in years."

"Perhaps you can choose a word other than 'comrade', doctor."

"Yes, yes. Of course." And they both laughed just as Elizabeth knocked at my study door.

After Elizabeth satisfied herself as to my safety and saw how sincerely happy Reilly and I were, she left us in peace once again with a twinkling, "Please don't get too rowdy. We wouldn't want to disturb our nice neighbours, now, would we?"

I then began to relate all that happened to me and Holmes and the Romanovs after Reilly had taken leave of us in Russia.

I told him of our voyage to the island, of our becoming settled and happy, of the hurricane, of the birth of baby Sidney, and of everyone's health when I departed on the fifth of July. It seemed so long ago, but had only been less than a month since I left Eleuthera.

Then, after a very deep breath, I told him of the supposed death of Holmes and Yardley and Preston, their homeward-bound ship supposedly sunk by the Germans. I told him of the visit of the man with the red beard and what he had told me: that "they" whoever "they" are, had Holmes in their captivity and if I wrote of his last great adventure serving his King and country in the Great War, Holmes would remain alive. If not, he would disappear "like coins the hands of a cheap magician."

I told him of the killing of Newsome, of my direct meeting with Lloyd George. I told of my meeting with Clay who had gone off to discover if Holmes was still alive, and of my promise to dramatize Clay's own death at the hands of disgruntled henchmen, which I did in "Feet of Clay", so that he could adopt another identity and be free.

"So Holmes may still be alive somewhere?" he asked.

"I most fervently hope so."

I then took from one of my desk drawers a sheaf of newspaper clippings I had saved about Holmes' heroic death and then my own deceitful tale of his death.

Finally, I told of the visit of my smaller nanny who had come to repay a favour Holmes and I had done for his family, by unspooling the web woven by Lloyd George and what I had dubbed "the Black Faction". But Reilly knew nothing of a red-bearded man and his tale of Holmes still being alive.

Now, spent myself, I said to Reilly, "I've told you everything, I believe. But I've not the mind to decipher the puzzles that you and Holmes find so elementary. Other than Holmes, I cannot think of another, but you, who I would expect to untangle this Gordian's knot."

He said not one word, at first, but sat immobile looking into my eyes. But I saw wheels turning behind them, as I had so often in Russia.

Finally, he spoke. "Watson, while I appreciate my equation with Holmes, our minds work in a very different manner. Holmes' mind divines the mystery, my mind devises it. I've listened very carefully to all you've just said, but until I have the time to ponder this at length, I have no answer or assurance of Holmes' fate to give you.

"However, our government has separate divisions, which, ironically, remain divided in every respect. One will work against the good of the other so that it may be more successful even though it may cost England most dear.

"As you may suspect, I have my resources both within and without, government which I will use to the utmost. But, Watson, as much as I truly wish to aid you about Holmes, I wish to see my wife and baby even more. I'm going to see them first, before anything else."

And though he immediately saw my desperate disappointment, he heard me

quietly say, "I understand. I do." I then gave him the secret and detailed information he would need to find Tatiana, baby Sidney and the Romanovs at the compound on Winding Bay.

As Reilly left me, with one hand holding hard my right and his other on my shoulder, he said, "John, for the good of your family, if only the loyal, loving hound could but turn into a jackal."

With that he was gone. And I could not have known at that moment that the faint words of hope he had given me about Holmes were nothing more than gossamer comfort.

I was not to hear from him until he appeared once again at my door, more than two years later.

"To paraphrase Machiavelli, 'Hold your friends close and your enemies closer'," said Holmes.

"I ain't holdin' nobody close but dollies," smirked Siegel.

"Will you shuddup and listen to the man," said Lansky as he playfully hit Siegel in the back of his head.

"Charlie," Holmes said, "you must meet with Masseria and offer him fealty."

"Huh?" Siegel asked.

"It means, Benny," Luciano said, "that I gotta go to Masseria and tell him that we're all gonna be workin' for him. We're gonna be soldiers for him."

"No way, no way I'm gonna work for that fat, greaseball, dago bag of crap."

"Calm down, Benny and listen," Lansky cautioned again.

"Ben," said Holmes as calmly a parent would when trying to teach a child to obey, "you're not really going to be working for him. You must make him believe that you and Meyer and Charlie can be trusted. Then, when he's lulled into false security, he can be dealt with."

"Dealt with? What's dealt with?" asked Siegel, only a bit more calmly.

"We can kill him," Luciano said.

"Now, that I understand. Yeah, I'll deal with him, all right," and Siegel pulled out the pistol he had in his pants.

"Put it away, putz," said Lansky.

"And just how do I convince him that Ben and Meyer and me and the rest of the guys with us are gonna be working for him?"

"Quite simple, really. Bring him a bag full of money. A very large bag filled with money. In ancient times it was called an offering. One gave a valuable gift to prove one's oath of fealty."

"Money's no problem," said Lansky. "How much do you think we should give?"

"Large enough to wet his appetite and that by working for him, you'll be able to bring him much more. Now be sure to have your pistols with you. You'll be searched anyway and if you came without your weapons, they would think something is awry. And don't become alarmed when they rummage through the money in your bag. They'll just to be sure there are no weapons hidden inside."

"Can't you talk English," said a frustrated Siegel.

"Yes, I can. Can you?" answered Holmes in jest.

But though both Lansky and Luciano expected some usually demented outburst by Siegel, he just reared his head back, slapped his knee and said, "Good one, Johnny, good one."

"Anything else?" asked Luciano.

"Yes. No matter what he demands of you, agree. Most assuredly he's going to demand too much. That will be a test. Hesitate, negotiate. If you give in immediately to his demands he'll know you're lying; and all three of you might as well dig your graves right there.

"And Ben, though you and Meyer will be separated from Charlie by Masseria's men, please don't become worried. They'll do no harm to him unless Masseria doesn't believe him. But, of course, Charlie will make him believe him."

"Done," said Luciano.

The very next day, Luciano, along with Lansky and Siegel, went to meet Masseria at one of his favorite restaurants, Nuova Villa Tammaro in Coney Island, Brooklyn. Outside the front door, and after all three men were frisked , as the Americans say, by one of Masseria's guards, Luciano was told to follow him inside to Masseria's table, but Lansky and Siegel were detained by other guards.

Remembering Holmes' injunction, Siegel's only outward sign of discontent was his incessant smoking and an almost involuntary walking in circles. This, however, because of Siegel's reputation, was looked upon with humor by

Masseria's guards, one of whom muttered under his breath, "Crazy, kike."

Though both Siegel and Lansky heard the remark, before Siegel erupted, Lansky had grabbed his arm, looked straight into his eyes, as he had hundreds of times before in their young lives, and willed Siegel to calm down and continue walking in his ceaseless circles.

Luciano was walked through what appeared to be the normal Italian restaurant of the day in lower New York. A large dark, oak bar was to the right, with a few small tables with red and white checkered tablecloths to the left. Then they walked through two frosted-glass doors to a private room. There were guards seated at tables to the right and left rear, with a large center table where sat Giuseppe, "Joe the Boss", Masseria.

"Sit," said Masseria.

Masseria was much overweight and slovenly. His tie and shirt were already soiled by some sauce earlier spilled. To Luciano's polished esthetic, learned from Rothstein, Masseria resembled nothing more than a particularly repulsive pig.

As Luciano sat, he handed over the satchel with the money.

Masseria wiped his mouth with his right hand, then onto the table cloth.

"I see you brought me a present and it ain't even my boithday?" With this he laughed uproariously, as did the guards.

"I bring this for you, Don Masseria, as a gesture of good will from me and my men."

"And why should you bring me such a present?" Masseria leaned over the table, as far as he could to be as close to Luciano as possible. Luciano knew that the next few words out of his mouth might be the most important he had ever spoken. Or might be his last.

"Because, Don Masseria, with Mr. Rothstein gone, you or Don Maranzano will take over everything. And me and boys are bettin' on you."

Masseria's eyes betrayed a mild glint of acceptance of those words, but still bore into Luciano.

"And why do you and your boys think that?"

"Because of the way you took over Don Rasata's territory; and we think you got bigger guns than Maranzano. You both want each other dead and we can help you make him dead. If you know anything about me and my boys you know plenty about what happened to Numbers Malone and his guys. And you know about Benny Siegel."

"That Bugsy of yours. Yeah, I know about that crazy Jew."

"Don Masseria, with all due respect, that crazy Jew is gonna kill Maranzano and keep you living. Nobody will know we're working for you. So Ben and Meyer and them other Jew guys we got, will kill Maranzano and it will be the Jewish gang that did it. The heat'll be off you. Then the whole thing will be yours."

"Yeah, how come you work with Jews? Our thing is Sicilian. I don't like it that you work with Jews."

"Again, with all due respect, Don Masseria. You like money, right? What do you care where it comes from? Or who gets it for you?

Masseria leaned back in his chair.

Luciano then told him a story he knew Masseria would totally understand.

"Don Masseria, I know you know of the Roman Emperor Vespasian," and he paused.

Masseria made a face as if to say, "Of course, I do."

Luciano continued, "Well, he gets in a bind for dough and he comes up with a real good idea. He puts a tax on the public toilets and the dough starts comin' in.

"Well, his advisors don't like that. It ain't proper t'collect money like that. So Vespasian, he calls over his top advisor guy, holds a coin under his nose and asks him if he smells anything?"

It took Masseria a few moments to finally understand, but even though he's smiling, he says, "I still don't like it; but as long as nobody is gonna know they're working for me, okay." What he said next, however, really took Luciano aback.

"Now the first thing I want you to do is go to Maranzano and tell him the same exact thing you just told me?

"Say that again, Don Masseria?" asked Luciano.

"You heard me. You ain't deaf. Now move. And I don't want to see you again

until Maranzano is dead. Dead!" Masseria stood up now, shouting, "Dead! I want him dead!"

Luciano stood, bowed his head crisply to Masseria, and walked out of the room. He still heard him shouting as he got to the front door of the restaurant where Lansky and Siegel were waiting. Siegel abruptly stopped walking in circles.

All were given back their weapons, got into their auto and drove off.

"So what was all that yelling about?" Lansky asked.

"Nothing much. He just wants me to tell Maranzano what I just told him."

"Wait till Johnny hears about this," Siegel said, laughing.

Holmes Meets A Tourist In New York

In Liverpool one day later, Reilly, still traveling as Roland Windsor, booked passage on RMS *Olympic*, the queen of the White Star Line and, at the time, the largest ocean liner in the world. She would leave the next day.

Olympic had served nobly in the Great War as a troop ship, but was recently reconverted to her passenger grandeur; she was the swiftest way in which to reach New York, a leisurely five days. From there, Reilly had already booked passage on a ship to take him to the Bahamas, *SS Brookland*, an American cargo ship accepting a significant number of passengers, as well.

As promised, a few hours passed five days, Reilly was in New York on August 9. Though he had been all over the world, he was not quite prepared for the sheer electric air of Manhattan.

While London was the center of the Empire and the world, New York seemed to be the veritable center of dynamic energy. While London could boast historic architecture, nothing there could compare with the new "skyscrapers", as they were being called. The Woolworth Building, the tallest of all, built in 1913, stood an incredible fifty-seven stories. At that time, one could get a nose bleed just thinking about the height.

Reilly had two days to pass while he waited for the final stage of his journey to begin to the Bahamas. And it was early on his second day in Manhattan, while his head stretched upward, straining to look at the top of the Woolworth Building, as all tourists did, that he thought he heard a familiar voice speaking his name, but in a question, "Reilly?"

Upon turning to see who would be addressing him so, he saw a tall, elderly man standing directly before him. The man was dressed in the mode of the day, expensively, too, Reilly noted. But immediately suspicious, Reilly reverted to SIS mode.

"Are you addressing me, sir?"

"I surmise my disguise has once again gotten the best of you. Just something I'm toying with at the moment."

Holmes was dressed in the usual gentleman's apparel, but with his new facial hair and color it would have been quite impossible to recognise him at hurried glance.

"I'm sure I don't know what you mean. Now good day, sir." But as Reilly turned to leave, the man gently, but firmly, grabbed his arm, turning Reilly back to face him.

"Oh, come, come Colonel Relinsky, don't you recognise me?" And Holmes winked at Reilly.

One closer look and, "What the devil? Holmes?"

"Your hearing is, at least, as good as ever," said Holmes. "But come with me where we can sit and quietly speak without this incessant New York noise."

Reilly said nothing, but continued to examine Holmes as he led them into a corner café directly opposite the Woolworth Building. Holmes chose a table towards the rear and they sat.

Though each shared the exceptional privilege of an incalculably keen mind, it seemed that neither could entirely digest the simple circumstance of the other's existence at that particular moment.

"This is unbelievable, Holmes. Quite unbelievable. The world thinks you're dead at the hands of the Huns. At least, most of the world."

"And so I shall remain, Reilly, so I shall remain. But you're wrong about this being unbelievable. The odds that you and I should meet like this here, now, are nothing short of astronomical."

"No, Holmes, you don't understand. I saw Dr. Watson at his home before I left for New York. What he told me was so incredible that I'm still sorting through it. But it concerned information of life and death for you. Perhaps you'll understand and be able to make sense of it."

He then told Holmes everything I had told him. And now Holmes knew, or thought he knew, who was responsible for his attempted murder; Lloyd George. Holmes would now be able to devise an appropriate revenge.

Reilly continued.

"Holmes, Watson is sick with worry about you.

"Poor Watson."

"I've got to let him know you're alive."

Holmes cut him short with a stringent command, "No. Under no circumstances must he know that."

"But Holmes, that's inhuman. The man loves you like a brother and should be told."

"Surely, Reilly, I don't have to explain why he cannot be made aware."

Reilly understood after a moment's thought and nodded acquiescence.

"Agreed," Reilly said, "though I'll feel that I've betrayed the trust of a man who deserves better. "

"Well, I am equally sure that this is an experience not unknown to you." The remark was biting and cut to Reilly's very being.

For a long moment Reilly stared hard into the impassive face of the Holmes that sat before him, but realized the words were true.

"Yes," he said quietly, then abruptly changed the subject to an immediate matter.

"Holmes, what did happen to you and why this disguise?"

"I will explain presently, but what about you?" Holmes' demeanor now shifted to the guise of old friend, though Reilly saw through it to its harsh marrow.

"My word, it is so good to see you alive, as well. What happened to you after you left us? What devilish plot had SIS devised for you back then?"

"I propose a truce," said Reilly. "I'll tell you my tale once you've told me yours."

Large pots of tea and pastry were ordered, and with much tea downed between them, each told of all that had happened subsequent to their last time together; with Holmes' account of his hopes for a criminal alliance disturbing Reilly greatly. Since Reilly was fully aware of Holmes' penchant for disguise in certain circumstances, Holmes did not need to explain further.

"How," asked Reilly, "do you propose Watson chronicle what we've just told each other? If ever he's able."

"Precisely," said Holmes. "For the tale to be truly told, I must succeed in what I must do."

Reilly leaned in closer. "Holmes, this criminal business of yours; I don't quite understand why you've not only allied with these murderers, but are giving them the blessing of your intellect."

"I will need them when I return to London. Clay's men there are hard, but there is a steel-hard malignancy among these American thugs that cannot be duplicated. I will need that.

"And besides, if one group of criminals do away with another group of criminals, so much less the tasks for the police here and in England. And I shall always be many steps ahead of them all, wherever they may be."

The words and Holmes' demeanor unsettled Reilly greatly. Holmes' whole being had darkened, even without his latest disguise.

"Holmes, you don't need those men. I can help you. Men I know and trust can help you. But you must wait till after I've returned."

"Reilly, I don't know when you'll return, of if you'll return and my business here will be concluded shortly. I most probably will be back in London while you're still in Eleuthera. I will need these men." He said this emphatically and with finality.

"I cannot steer you from this course?"

"Not Jove, himself."

"Then I can only wish you luck and my hand. You know that if our paths cross again, and I hope they do, I'll aid in any way I'm able."

"I trust that you will. Good luck to you. Please give my regards to Tatiana and her family. As to your baby, I wish him a long, happy life."

But to Reilly, these words seemed nothing more than perfunctory. Any sincerity to be detected in the eyes of someone saying those words was not there. All that showed was a cold, blank stare.

With that, Reilly left Holmes sitting at the table and walked out of the cafe. Once outside, he stopped as if to return, then stopped himself from doing so. As much as he would have wanted to aid Holmes, he wanted to see his wife and baby even more. He also had the unsettling feeling that the man inside did not seem to be Holmes anymore. So he continued his tour of Manhattan.

In his unaccustomed role as tourist, Reilly failed to notice a man looking at him while he was looking at the buildings. It was the same man who had been watching him since that night in Helsinki.

Luciano Gets The Once Over Twice

Luciano's meeting with Maranzano went according to plan. Maranzano seemed more polished than Masseria, but only barely. He certainly dressed better, in Luciano's keen sartorial eye, but he had a perpetual look of disdain that just further raised Luciano's ire.

Maranzano seemed happy to have Luciano and his men come under his thumb. It would make it that much easier to do away with Masseria and become the capo di tutti capi, the boss of all bosses.

But two days after that meeting, as Luciano strolled long his familiar streets of the lower east side of Manhattan alone, a large black motor car stopped at the curb beside him. Two men jumped out of the car and pushed Luciano into the rear, at pistol point; one on either side of him.

"What's with the gats, guys? I was just takin' a walk."

The man to the right of Luciano had already removed Luciano's revolver from his jacket and then quickly searched him for any other weapons that may have been hidden; but found none. He nodded to the other man that Luciano was "clean".

The man to the left, answered Luciano. "Nope, Charlie. We're takin' ya for a ride." This, in American gangster slang meant they were going to kill him.

What happened next was nothing less than inhuman. The men blindfolded Luciano and tied his hands. Though it seemed that they were driving for a long period of time, Luciano could not tell just how long. He further felt that the auto was on the water and thought, "Holy crap, they're gonna kill me in Jersey and dump me out there somewhere."

Then he felt they were back on a road and when the auto stopped, he was pulled out of the auto and he heard what sounded like a warehouse door sliding open. He was walked inside, pushed down into a chair and tied to that chair.

When the blindfold was removed, Luciano could see that he was, indeed, inside

what looked like a bare warehouse. There were three big and beefy men looking at him as they removed their suit jackets. Luciano suspected what would happen next.

The biggest of the men spoke first.

"So, Charlie, how ya doin'?"

Luciano gave a laugh-grunt. "Okay, guys, what do ya wanna know?"

"I don't wanna know nothin'. You guys wanna know anythin'?" The two other men shook their heads.

"Ya see, Charlie, we already know everythin' we need t' know. What we want you t' know is this." And with that, he punched Luciano hard in his right eye, which began to bleed profusely.

The second man stepped forward. He had a knife in his hand. "And this." He stabbed Luciano numerous times in the chest; but not deeply.

The third man stepped forward. He had a tyre chain in his hand. "Oh, yeah, and this." He hit Luciano across his shins. But Luciano was already unconscious.

He regained his senses as water lapped at his battered head and body. He found himself on a beach. He was in excruciating pain and blind in his right eye. His bonds had been untied and all he could do was crawl a few inches.

"Hey, mister, you okay?" Of all people, a police officer had found him.

"Help me," said Luciano. He could barely make the sound, but enough for the officer to hear and then to summon an ambulance to take him to the nearest hospital.

Luciano was in Staten Island, the least populated borough of New York City, mostly still undeveloped and considered another planet by most other New Yorkers. So out of the way was its location, in fact, that the only way to reach Staten Island at this time was by ferry boat from the foot of Manhattan or by train.

The police questioned him thoroughly, but for once, what he told the police was the absolute truth: he didn't know who the men were who beat him, where he had been taken, what they wanted, nor how he wound up on that beach in Staten Island. And since it was difficult for Luciano to speak, the police ceased their interrogation at the order of the physicians.

Though professionally skeptical of any criminal's statements, there wasn't much they could do. There was no need to leave officers outside Luciano's room, because if those men had wanted him dead, he would already be so. So the police left. It wasn't long after the police had departed before Lansky, Siegel and a few of their men arrived. Luciano had asked the nurses to ring Lansky.

When Lansky and Siegel entered Luciano's room, the other men were posted outside, they couldn't believe what lay before them. Most of Luciano was encased in bandages. But he was awake and aware. Lansky held back tears. Even Siegel was sickened at what he saw. Yet he still quipped, "Jesus Christ, Charlie, who turned you into a mummy?"

Though it was difficult to speak, Luciano said, "Very funny, Ben."

It was Lansky who spoke next. "Enough. No more talkin' for Charlie. He gotta get strong and rest. Charlie, we're gonna take you home as soon as you're okay, but I gotta ask, who did this. Don't talk, just nod or somethin'." Luciano shrugged his shoulders.

"You really don't know?" asked Lansky. Luciano very slowly shook his head "no".

It was Siegel's turn. "One thing, the minute I find out who did this, they're dead."

"We know that, Benny. Charlie, we had to come to see you just to be sure you're okay. We'll leave a couple of the guys outside just in case, but we'd never of heard from you again if those guys wanted you dead." Luciano nodded assent.

"Take it easy, Charlie. You look good," laughed Siegel as they walked out.

"Don't worry about anything, Charlie. We got you covered. We'll talk with Clay about this, too. Gey shluffin," Lansky said as he walked out. Those last words were Yiddish for "go to sleep."

On the ride back to Manhattan, Lansky turned to Siegel seated next to him in the rear. "I didn't want Charlie t' know, but this can really spell trouble. When we're back we'll get a hold of Clay. I got some ideas of what happened and I wanna go over them with you and him."

"Good," Siegel said. "But I just wanna make somebody dead."

Sidney Reilly Meets Sidney Reilly

Even though Reilly had been exquisitely trained to bury feelings and emotions when on assignment, he was not on assignment now. He had just boarded the *Brookland* and he actually believed he felt the proverbial butterflies in his stomach. And, he thought, if he felt this way now, just how would he feel gazing upon Tatiana once again, and little Sidney, for the first time?

Normally, it would take about two days from New York to Nassau, but with its stops along the way to deliver and pick up cargo, it would take *Brookland* four. Then a few more hours by local boat or ferry to Eleuthera. To Reilly, the incongruity of a mere four days equating with the eternity of four days caused him to smile to himself.

At last, he was in Nassau and he wasted no time in securing a small, private boat to bring him to Eleuthera, which would take only two to three hours. Once docked, with the instructions and directions I had given him, Reilly knew it best for him to walk to the Romanov compound on Winding Bay, and not to hire a conveyance to bring him there. He arrived in another hour's time.

He skirted the main path of the house and slowly walked up the gentle incline to the right, eyes fixed on the house for any sign of the Romanovs and trusting his peripheral vision to alert him of anyone else.

There were busy workers who seemed to pay him no mind. But there was one who watched from the shade of a banana tree as Reilly passed by. The man followed quietly from some distance without Reilly knowing, so intent was Reilly on seeing Tatiana and Sidney.

Then, as he passed the main house and could see around to the rear, he let out an audible gasp. There, not fifty feet away, were Tatiana, baby Sidney, and the Grand Duchesses. Marie was tickling Sidney on a large white blanket while Tatiana and the others were watching and laughing as baby Sidney, only six months old, laughed.

It was Anastasia who spied Reilly first, and as had just happened with Reilly, she let out a gasp. Tatiana, Marie and Olga looked at Anastasia, then looked in the direction that she was looking and all gave out loud gasps.

Tatiana seemed frozen as she stood staring at Reilly; as frozen as was he. Then they ran at each other with ecstatic velocity. That was the precise term used by Reilly when he told me about their reunion.

The man watching Reilly simply turned and went back to his spot under the banana tree.

The Grand Duchesses were all now crying, as were Tatiana and Reilly. All, but baby Sidney who may have sensed his father's presence and was laughing loudly as Reilly lifted him in his arms, high against the azure Eleutheran sky and quietly said, "My son, my son. If only you knew how much I love you."

Tatiana took hold of Reilly's shoulders as he held baby Sidney and laughed and cried as she repeated, "Your father is home, your father is home." Then, to herself, "You are home, you're here."

Marie went to take baby Sidney from Reilly so that he and Tatiana could further embrace and kiss, but Tatiana pushed her away gently. "No, Marie, let the father and son be together. Let them feel each other. Let them love."

It was at this point that the Tsar and the Tsarevich, Alexei, now quite a young man of fifteen, came out of the main house and were also taken aback at what they saw.

Alexei, once again not thinking as he should to protect himself, went running to the happy group. Luckily, there was no incident. As Tatiana scooped up baby Sidney from Reilly, Alexei held Reilly in the tightest hug he could muster as he proudly whispered, "Reilly. Pretty strong now, huh?"

"And who is this man holding my grandson so?" asked the Tsar with an immense grin and dressed as a peasant of the fields; which he had loved to do in the gardens of the Livadia Palace at Yalta.

"It's Reilly, Papa; don't you recognise him?" Alexei asked, in a now more mature and masculine voice.

"Of course, I do, of course, I do," the Tsar said as he gently patted Alexei's back. "My word, Colonel, how did you get here? Are you all right?" asked the Tsar as he gave Reilly the two kiss greeting.

"Father," said Tatiana, "please, not now. I'm sure there will be plenty of time for Sidney to tell us everything. But for now, I just want to be alone with him and our son. And that means you, too Alexei. Don't bother him now."

With that, Tatiana put her arm around Reilly's waist and they walked away from the house, away from the Tsar, away from the Tsarevich, away from the Grand Duchesses, across the beautiful lawn and sat on a bench facing the sea. Away from the entire world.

Alexei joined the Grand Duchesses who had stopped their happy crying and were now just smiling at the reunited family. The Tsar returned to the house.

In a beautiful, white and lavender solarium, facing that same serene sea, the sun illuminating the room till it glowed as if in a fairy tale, the Tsar went to sit with the Tsarina. He took her hands in his as she sat staring blankly out the window, her once-thick chestnut hair now almost completely gray.

"Sonny. Sonny," the Tsar gently said, calling her by his loving nickname for her. "Reilly is here. He's come back. He's with Tatiana and baby Sidney."

The Tsarina turned her face to him, but her expression was still blank. She was sinking father into her own, deep dimension.

How Lucky Can You Get?

Once back on home territory, Lansky and Siegel sat down with Holmes at a table in Lansky's trucking company office. Lansky reported on the state of Luciano's health and what had happened to him.

"From what you've described," said Holmes, "Charlie is lucky to be alive."

"Hey, that's good. That's real good," said Siegel laughing. "From now on Charlie is gonna be 'Lucky'. Lucky Luciano. I bet he's really gonna like that."

"I think he's gonna like it better if you call him Charlie, like always," reasoned Lansky.

"So, John, I got some ideas on what happened, but I'd like to hear what you think," Lansky said to Holmes.

"Yes, well, from what you've related, we have a number of possible scenarios and one overarching question which may provide an answer: why was Charlie left alive?"

"Yeah, that's the big question. Like I said, I have my ideas but I wanna hear yours."

"Me, too," said Siegel.

"All right, then, these are my thoughts. If Maranzano suspected Charlie of duplicity, what happened was a message delivered that he could be killed whenever Maranzano chose. But he was left alive because Maranzano wasn't entirely sure; and if Charlie were telling the truth about serving him, then he was certainly worth more alive than dead. And now he would truly fear Maranzano.

"If it was Masseria who had this done, the same holds true. Which leaves us with a rather profound conundrum."

"What's this conderbum crap?" Siegel asked.

"It's a puzzle, a riddle. And right now, it looks like none of us can solve it," Lansky said.

"Unfortunately," said Holmes.

Upon that, it seemed as if stilted silence had taken sway. Lansky and Holmes could do nothing but look at each other, as if by that simple act one of them might deduce why what happened, happened.

"One thing's definite, though," Siegel said, "since we can't be sure who did that to Charlie, they both gotta die. And the sooner the better because I don't wanna end up like Charlie or worse and I don't think that either of you do, too."

"I believe that Ben has grasped the central point quite nicely," Holmes said.

"Yeah, I agree. We'll start planning this now, but we don't do nothin' till Charlie's back," Lansky said.

"That would be most efficacious," agreed Holmes.

"Goddammit, Johnny, can't you just talk English?" asked Siegel with some exasperation.

"Hey, I don't even know that word," said Lansky with a smile and a shrug, easing the tension.

"It means that you are one hundred percent correct, Meyer. Your idea is the most efficient for our purposes."

"Great. I can't wait for Charlie to get back," said Siegel.

Holmes then got up from his chair, went to a large cabinet he knew was used to house Meyer's alcohol, retrieved some glasses and some scotch and returned to the table, setting the glasses carefully down in front of Lansky and Siegel, with one where he would be sitting. He then proceeded slowly to pour the scotch into each glass, never taking his eyes off the scotch as it fell, circled the table and sat, head down, looking at his glass of scotch.

At first, Lansky thought Holmes' actions odd, but then realized he was in the grip of a plan and that he needed those simple movements to help him formulate that plan. Holmes then lifted his head, looked at Lansky, then Siegel.

"Now, I don't want you gentlemen to think I have lost my sanity, but this is how I believe we should proceed," Holmes said.

Neither Lansky nor Siegel said a word, so intent to hear what Holmes had next to say.

"You are going to dispense with them both at the same time. I don't mean precisely at the same time, but one right after the other. Within a very few hours." Siegel and Lansky looked at each other.

Siegel spoke first. "Johnny, you know I think you got brains like Meyer, but how we gonna kill those guys on the same day with all the muscle they got?"

"Yeah, John," said Lansky, "it seems like we might be bitin' off more than we can chew."

Holmes smiled and said, "That depends on where you bite."

After convalescing for two weeks, Luciano was discharged. He was met by Lansky and Siegel in his room and a half dozen of their men at the entrance. Now that the bandages were completely removed, they noticed a nasty scar on his right cheek and that his right eyelid was drooping badly. But they said nothing.

As Luciano left the hospital, the men greeted him heartily with:

"Hey, Lucky; glad you're back!"

"Good t' see ya, Lucky!"

"Ya never looked better, Lucky!"

Luciano turned to Lansky, "What's with all this 'Lucky' crap?" Siegel gave a big laugh. Lansky said, "Get in the car, Charlie, and I'll tell you what's up."

By the time they were safe in Luciano's sumptuous apartment in the Waldorf Towers a few hours later, one of Manhattan's most posh residences, in fact one in which one of America's ex-presidents, Herbert Hoover, would call home later, Luciano had been completely briefed by Lansky in such detail that even napkin colors were mentioned, so thorough were the preparations. All venues had been scouted and every contingency planned for.

Charlie agreed that according to Holmes' plan, they would move ahead the very next day. Holmes came to pay his respects a few hours after their return.

"I must say that it's truly good to see you again, Charlie. I hope that eye isn't causing you any trouble."

"Nah. Just makes me look half sleepy; but both eyes are always open. It's good t' see you, too. Please sit. Johnny, I like your plan; Meyer filled me in."

"With even a modicum of luck, you should succeed," Holmes said, reassuringly.

"Yeah, that's exactly what I think," said Luciano.

"But I've added a twist, Charlie," Holmes said, as all now gave full attention to Holmes. "I expanded on the plan, and I'd like to discuss it now with all of you."

"We're all ears," Siegel said, flapping both of his with his hands.

Holmes then laid out his expanded plan as all sat and listened.

When Holmes had finished, all Siegel could do was give out with an elongated whistle. Lansky just sat, the permutations going through his mind as quickly as a roulette ball spinning in the wheel.

Of them all, it was Luciano who grasped the true significance of the plan's audacity, and what it would mean for him and his closest allies.

"John, obviously you know what this will do for me and Meyer and Ben and our guys ?" Luciano asked, but was really making a statement.

"Of course I do. But no matter what should happen today, I believe it imperative you move as soon as you make the arrangements. Hopefully within a week," Holmes said.

"I can't wait," Siegel said, exhibiting that eccentric back-and-forth rocking motion of his.

"Most assuredly," Holmes said.

"Ben, get us some glasses and booze, huh?" Luciano asked.

"No problem. I could use a belt right now, anyway," Siegel said.

When their glasses had been filled, the four of them stood in a circle and Luciano toasted.

"Domani, guys, Domani!"

"Domani!"

"Domani!"

Domani

Domani came. It was November 5, 1919.

Masseria greeted Luciano at the same table of the same restaurant in which they'd first met; and as at that first meeting, Masseria was eating lustily. Luciano sat down opposite Masseria when gestured to do so.

"Too bad that, Charlie," said Masseria, as he made a motion with his knife across his cheek. Luciano wasn't sure if it was a mocking gesture or simply an imitative one. "So tell me, what happened? I hear they're calling you 'Lucky' now. I like that. Lucky Luciano. So tell me, what happened?"

Luciano began to unfold the tale, but after a few minutes, he looked uncomfortable and said to Masseria, "Don Masseria, you must forgive me, but after this happened, I gotta go t' the bathroom a lot. Do you mind?"

"What do I care? I certainly don't want you to piss all over the floor right here." He laughed, expecting the bodyguards who were usually there to laugh with him. But they weren't there. And he didn't notice, or seem to care, as he dug his fork deep into a dish of spaghetti and meatballs.

It took only a minute or two after Luciano entered the bathroom before he heard the pistols discharging. Many pistols discharging. When they stopped, he slowly walked back to where Masseria had been sitting. He was now splayed out on the floor with the table on top of him, meatballs and blood everywhere. But he still held a fork in his hand.

The first part of Lansky's plan had been carried out perfectly by Siegel, Reles and Buchalter.

Three hours later, in midtown Manhattan, on the ninth floor of the Helmsley Building, an office door burst open and three police officers charged in with pistols drawn. The two guards in the outer office wouldn't stop the police and handed over their weapons as soon as directed to do so.

The other two policemen went into the inner office, that of Salvatore Maranzano. He rose immediately from his desk, went around and addressed them in a calm manner.

"Officers, officers, I'm sure this must be a misunderstanding. You know your captain and me are friends and that..." He didn't finish the sentence as one of the police officers stabbed him. The other officer shot him three times.

When the guards outside heard the pistol shots, they rushed the first officer but he shot them dead before they could reach him.

The officers were, in reality, the same cast as in Coney Island; Siegel, Reles and Buchalter.

That night, across the United States, many of the old Mustache Petes met similar fates; as they were shot, stabbed, garroted, or made to disappear through other means of local disposal. The American tabloids, looking for one all-encompassing sensational phrase, called it "The Night of the Sicilian Vespers".

In one horrific night, a new group of young gangsters had emerged to take command of the American underworld; and Charlie "Lucky" Luciano emerged as the most powerful gangster in the country.

The plan that Holmes had devised and to which Lansky and Luciano had given their blessing, had been accomplished purely, perfectly and with clinical precision. Holmes smiled to himself. He had chosen these allies most wisely, indeed.

The plan to organize the disparate criminal groups was presented by Luciano and Lansky at a meeting of all the bosses, after Holmes had returned to London; but taken from a simple idea that he had proposed: conduct your business as would any American corporation.

The men who led various gangs in the cities across the country were now heads of

"families;" the capo, or boss. And each capo of each family sat at the corporate table and had an equal vote.

Luciano would act as a kind of chairman of the board and ultimate arbiter of disagreements between these families if they could not be resolved peacefully among themselves. Gang warfare was bad for business. Too much heat from the press, the politicians and the police. Better to buy them all off and have them in your pocket.

Luciano was the capo di tutti capi. The boss of all bosses.

Lansky, however, was more of a member emeritus because he was Jewish; and only Italians, preferably Sicilians, were members of this syndicate. To Italians, it was La Cosa Nostra, literally "our thing".

Yet, these men who disdained him as a Jew, listened when Lansky spoke and almost universally heeded his advice. This was not because Luciano and Lansky were so close, but for the simple reason that Lansky was usually right. And he could always be trusted.

Siegel was just a feared and powerful underling. He answered to Luciano, Lansky and the syndicate. He was nothing more than an angry bee who could sting, but who could also be swatted.

Holmes And Fairbanks And Pickford

All was now at the ready. It was the fourteenth of November and Holmes was taking leave of his rather unsavory associates in New York.

He had booked first class passage on RMS *Aquitania* and Luciano, Lansky and Siegel had personally brought Holmes down to *Aquitania* for his voyage back to London.

Upon their arrival, all were amused to literally encounter not one, but two brass bands and a multitude of people so densely packed together on the dock that Holmes' sardonic thought was that of sardines.

"What the hell?" Siegel asked. "This for us?"

Lansky, Luciano and Holmes had no idea why such an enraptured throng should be dockside until Holmes spied numerous signs with various sayings, such as "WE LOVE YOU MARY!", "WE LOVE YOU DOUG!", "CONGRATULATIONS!", "HAPPY HONEYMOON!", "COME BACK SOON!"

It seems that Holmes had booked passage on the very liner carrying the international motion picture stars from Hollywood, Mary Pickford and Douglas Fairbanks, on their honeymoon voyage to Europe.

As Pickford and Fairbanks made royal progress up the gangway, Siegel said, "Holy mackerel, wouldya get a load of those two. Holy cow! Hey, Johnny, that's our royalty," he laughed.

It was now time for Luciano, Lansky and Siegel to each give Holmes a personal goodbye.

Siegel said, "Take care, Johnny. We got a lot ridin' on ya. I forgot to ask all this time, they got Jews in England?"

"Yes, Ben, quite a few."

"Good. Hey, I just thought a somethin' funny, now get this: Eng-lish, Jew-ish. We're related by ishes." He laughed as he shook Holmes' hand and gave him a hug. "And don't hit no icebergs. Greenbergs, okay, though." He continued to laugh.

Lansky was next. "It was real interesting thinking with you, Johnny. I know you'll be keepin' tabs. And I know that you know that we'll be keepin' tabs, too. Gay mit mazel." Yiddish for "good luck." He, too, shook Holmes' hand and gave him a hug.

Luciano was last. "You done good helpin' us here. Now the big help comes. You gotta keep that booze comin', Johnny. We know you been makin' those arrangements with your guys in England. A couple more months and Prohibition kicks in. We're countin' on ya."

"No fear, Charlie. I need you as much as you need me. The first shipment of scotch will be delivered as planned to your boats off Long Island and then I'll wait for further instructions on when and where the next shall go."

"Right," Luciano paused, then leaned close to Holmes' ear and said, "Johnny, all that happened since Mr. Rothstein got bumped off, we owe it t' you. You planned everythin'. I don't know if we ever coulda done it without you.

"Buona fortuna, Johnny. I hope we can meet again." Then he took Holmes hand.

"I, as well, Charlie, I, as well." With that, Holmes turned and went up the gangway, turning one last time to wave down to the three men who were waving up.

Once settled into his stateroom, Holmes grasped that with Pickford and Fairbanks aboard, and with such lavish attention surely to be paid such Hollywood royalty, he could remain even more incognito. And so he would have been if not for an unfortunate event on the first night out.

It seems that while Holmes patrolled the deck in the silent morning hours, when all to attend one's ears were the sounds of the sea being pushed aside by the liner lithely slicing the waves, unable to sleep and pondering his actions when back in London, a door suddenly thrust open and a very inebriated, tiny woman came rushing out, quite unsteadily; and had not Holmes been there to come between her and the railing, the woman would have most certainly gone overboard.

As she tangled in Holmes' overcoat, a man came running out and instantly uncoupled her from Holmes, while trying to hold her up. It was Fairbanks and Pickford.

"I am so sorry to cause you this trouble," said Fairbanks, "unfortunately, Mary likes her spirits perhaps a bit too much for her own good." He hadn't even looked up at Holmes, just speaking while he tried to hold his wife upright as she went limp.

"No trouble, at all, I can assure you. It's a good thing I was here, however, or your wife would've become one with Neptune."

Fairbanks laughed. "Yes, that's a good one. Listen, pal, I know you've already done me a great favor just saving my wife's life, but do you think I could ask for another one?"

"What is it?" asked Holmes.

"I'd really appreciate it if you kept this under your hat. There's no need for anyone other than us to know what just happened; you get it? If the papers ever got wind of this, boy, oh, boy would they go haywire."

"Yes, I can easily see that. Of course, I'll keep silent. There's no reason for me tell anyone. "

"Hey, that's really great of you. I'll owe you big time." He was still holding Pickford in his arms as if she were nothing more than a doll, so small was she and so strong was he. "Say, pal, what's your name, anyway?" All this as he inched his way back to the door from which Ms. Pickford had so recently burst.

"Clay, John Clay."

"Well, John, I'll ask the captain to seat you at our table. It's the least I can do."

"Oh, please no; that's totally unnecessary."

"That may be," as he opened the door to go back inside, "but I always pay a debt. I just hope I don't bump into anyone on the way back to our stateroom. Our table isn't that big." With that, he laughed, the door closed and they were gone.

Holmes shrugged and continued his patrol of the deck.

The very next day as promised, a brief, personal invitation was slipped under his stateroom door.

"The captain requests the pleasure of your company for dinner tonight at this personal table. Dinner will be at eight precisely. Formal dress required."

"Oh, blast," thought Holmes, "I should have let her go over the side."

However, he attended and pretended.

He and the loving couple were the only guests of the captain on this particular night. Miss Pickford continued her unrelenting quest to quench her thirst, and Mr. Fairbanks made jokes, performed some sleight of hand to make playing cards disappear, and Holmes thought that Fairbanks would much rather have done the trick using his wife.

The captain was effusive in his praise and his toasts to his celebrated guests and Pickford seemed especially pleased with each toast. Not the words, but the implied invitation to raise one's glass again.

Fairbanks, having obviously seen this act before, and before Pickford could spoil the act, graciously suggested that they retire to their stateroom because he felt a tad under the weather.

"You go, Dougie," she said to her grimacing husband, literally pushing him at his chest, "I'm gonna stay here with the captain and Mr. Clay." She was slurring her words and sloshing her drink. The captain had now also realized the situation and very cleverly stated, "Oh, I hate to be one to stifle a party, but I've just received word that I'm urgently needed on the bridge."

"You got a bridge on this thing?" she asked. "Any trolls underneath?" It was now vibrantly evident that she was seriously snookered.

"Unfortunately, yes. You will excuse me." With that the captain left us as Fairbanks looked at me and shrugged his shoulders as if to say, "Now what?"

"Ah, well," Holmes said, winking to Fairbanks, "I believe I heard that there's an amazing party being held in stateroom number 180 and from what I hear, the champagne is flowing free and cold like the Atlantic outside."

"That's good enough for me," she said; and though she rose unsteadily and even with Fairbanks' aid walked awkwardly, they made it out of the dining hall, and Holmes supposed, back to their stateroom where, no doubt, Pickford would pass out and, hopefully, would remain in that state until morning.

As they left the table, Fairbanks held up his fingers indicated the number "two", as in "That makes two I owe you." However, Holmes felt he needed no more debts be repaid. He therefore devised a simple stratagem to avoid such repayment: as Fairbanks had been trying to do with the playing cards, he would disappear.

What this meant was that he would no longer appear for meals in the first-class dining room, he would, instead, frequent the second-class dining room and accommodations and keep to their deck, as well.

He would have succeeded in this newest transformation from Holmes to Clay to invisible man, except for the fact that on the fourth day, returning to his cabin after another brisk walk on the second-class deck, he found Fairbanks waiting for him.

"Hey, John, there you are!"

"Yes, indeed. Here I am."

"Where have you been, pal? I've been looking for you for days. I finally had to get the purser to give me your stateroom number so I could find you. Funny, I just got here and then you showed up. Talk about perfect timing."

"Or imperfect."

"Huh? Well, look. I owe you and I owe you big. So don't worry." He took out a paper and handed it to Holmes.

"I was gonna leave this for you when you showed up. It's very hush-hush, but I know you can keep a secret. It's where Mary and I will be in London. We're staying at the swankiest place in town, the Savoy. That musical fella, built it. You know, whatshizname, Coylie Dart or something like that?"

"You mean D'Oyly Carte?"

"Yeah, that's it! It's supposed to be the bees' knees! We have the bridal suite, of course, and I can't wait to see the joint."

"I'm sure you'll be suitably impressed. As will they."

"Yeah, and our ambassador is trying to get us in to see the King. He said the King's a big fan of ours. But then ain't everyone?"

"I have certainly not missed one of your epics."

"Yeah? Which one did you like the best?"

"The one where you rescued the girl." Of course, Holmes, to my knowledge, had never seen one of Fairbanks' motion pictures; but to Holmes, probably all had the swashbuckler rescuing some damsel devilishly imperiled.

"Yeah, that's swell. And here's our private phone number at Pickfair in Hollywood if you ever come over. You don't need an address, just jump in a cab. Everyone knows where Pickfair is. Hey, we might bump into Rudy if he's there, or Charlie. He's a Brit, too, so you two should have a lot to talk about."

He was speaking of Rudolph Valentino and Charlie Chaplin, of course. But to Fairbanks, though those two men were at the summit of international stardom and anyone other than Holmes would have immediately made arrangements to show up at the Pickfair doorstep, to Fairbanks, the names were toss-aways; simply friends and business associates.

"Thank you. I promise to contact you should I find myself in Hollywood," Holmes said.

"Great, great! And don't forget that we'll be in London for a few weeks before we head off to Paris, then we're off to do one of those Grand Tours all over Europe and we won't be back in London till after the new year some time. But keep that to yourself, too, okay?"

"Most assuredly."

"Great, great. Maybe we can even get together in London. Okay, hope to see you soon." And he was gone with that peripatetic pace for which Fairbanks was universally known and admired.

Once inside his stateroom, Holmes put the paper aside, sank into a chair and began to gather his thoughts, for he would be docking in London the next day. And his life as John Clay was about to begin in earnest.

Idyll In Eleuthera

After all the turmoil of Russia, the mayhem in Helsinki, the visit with Watson and hearing his disturbing story, this idyll in Eleuthera seemed so fragile, so ephemeral, as mere vapor which would dissipate in an instant.

Reilly had known no true surcease in his lifetime, and now he was truly sampling its mythic, unrelenting joy. His wife was more beautiful and loving than he even remembered and his son was the sun, itself.

Baby Sidney, at seven months, had the black hair of his mother, the silly disposition of his Aunt Anastasia, the playfulness of his Uncle Alexei, and the strength and stubbornness of his father.

There was the simple joy of experiencing family; though the Tsarina was still living in her own secluded world and growing more detached with each day.

Other than that one ever-expanding shadow, Reilly could not want for more. Every day he felt ancient tensions released from not only his body, but his mind. A life of duplicity and deceit and mistrust and murder was evaporating at his baby's tiny touch.

Tatiana knew better than to ask what had happened when he left them in Russia; at least for the moment. And the rest of the family was cautioned by her to just enjoy his presence and, as yet, not to seek answers to all the questions they so anxiously wanted to ask.

Finally, after two weeks of seamless tranquility, Reilly turned to Tatiana as they sat with baby Sidney on that big, beautiful white blanket in the soothing Eleutheran sun.

"Tatiana, thank you."

"For what?"

"For letting me just be and not poking and prodding and pestering me about where I was, who I was with, what happened; the usual answers a wife would demand from a gallivanting husband gone for over a year."

Rather than laughing, Tatiana took his face in her hands.

"I know how deeply you mean that, Sidney; though even now you must wrap your truest emotions in a jest. Someday I'll ask you about all that, but not now, not now. It's not important. What's important is that you're here with our son, with me. That we have each other to love again in every sense of the word. That the time flown between us didn't matter. It didn't lessen our love or keep us from each other's thoughts every moment of every day. "

Reilly simply reached over to pull Tatiana to him and they embraced as baby Sidney lay at their feet, happily asleep.

But Reilly knew that the time had come to give permission to the family to ask those certain questions. Tatiana had told him of the relationship that had blossomed between Marie and Yardley before he left with Holmes and that it might be best if he spoke to her privately before dinner that night; which he did.

He told Marie that as far as he knew, William Yardley had perished with Holmes. He felt it more beneficial for her to believe him dead than to recount what Holmes had told him in New York, that Yardley might have tried to murder Holmes.

At dinner that night, Reilly suddenly put down his knife and fork loudly, which interrupted a lively conversation between Anastasia and Alexei, turned his head slowly around the table and said, "Well, what are you waiting for?"

Alexei immediately knew what he meant, gave out with a yelp and then the Grand Duchesses and the Tsar understood, too. It was Alexei who spoke first, or, rather, let loose such a torrent of interrogation which would make magistrates of Her Majesty's High Court of Justice blush in admiration.

"So what happened when you left us? Did you kill any Bolshies? How did you kill them? How did you get here? Did King George send you on a big battleship?"

Reilly, laughing, and everyone else by now, as well, held up both his hands in abject surrender.

"I give up. Please, Alexei, no more. You overpower me with your questions."

"But you said I could ask."

"That's not precisely accurate. I simply indicated that I was ready to recount my grisly adventures." He stressed the word "grisly" with a menacing glee that had everyone laughing.

"You see. I was right. So tell us. How grisly?" Alexei asked.

"Oh, monsterously grisly. Tremendously grisly." Reilly was rising up from his chair and making threatening motions with his arms, waving them around wildly. Then he summarily slumped back into his chair and whispered to all, "Hideously grisly."

The Romanovs were all laughing but Reilly knew he would now have to invent a story to make them all happy. Grisly and not so grisly. So he began his fanciful fiction.

But one serious note before he began, he cautioned them all to never repeat one word of what he was about to divulge. This would make it seem that the fairy tale he was about to spin would be taken as gospel fact.

Outside, concealed in the lush vegetation and by the night, a man watched the standing Reilly gesticulating madly and saw a group of people he recognised, but could not believing he was actually seeing.

Introducing Mr. Stash

Holmes' feet touched English soil for the first time since June 1918. It was now November 19, 1919.

Involuntarily, he stood transfixed for a moment, akin to Antaeus in Greek mythology, who maintained his prodigious power by keeping his feet on the Earth; because Gaia, the mother of Earth was also his mother.

There were more brass bands and banners there to greet the honeymoon couple, but Holmes skirted them all. His belongings followed closely in two large steamer trunks, hauled by two specially engaged deckhands, and were deposited into the boot of a cab.

"I wish to go to the corner of Vallance Road and Lomas Street." Holmes said.

The driver turned around, looked Holmes up and down and said, "But that's in Shoreditch, in Whitechapel. It's full o' Fagins."

"I know where it is. I did not ask for a geography lesson. I asked to be taken there. Now."

"All right, guv', you're the boss, all right," and off they went.

As you are most certainly aware, this particular destination was not in the most desirable area of London. In fact, Whitechapel had spawned Jack the Ripper. And even at this time, few of proper means or personage would desire to dwell or do commerce within its environs.

The corner building, 13 Lomas Street, was a bestial building surrounded by other bestial buildings, in turn surrounded by more.

Clay had used this as a meeting place with his villains, believing that no one would think anyone as highborn as he to be at such a setting; and Holmes was now Clay.

He settled in.

The new year of 1920 arrived, but it was the sixteenth of January which meant the most to Holmes and his new-found friends in New York; for Prohibition had gone into effect in America.

Holmes, as Clay, had completed his criminal suzerainty before that date. All that had been Clay's was now Holmes' as Clay. No one knew that Clay no longer existed. All of Holmes' instructions would be delivered by underlings to other underlings.

These were not men of superior intellect; a certain criminal cunning, perhaps, but none who could complete a Sunday Times crossword puzzle. Or begin one. Or know what one was.

The sea-going, alcohol pipeline from Scotland to Long Island, New York had
been the first order of business for Holmes and it had gone as smoothly and efficiently as one would expect of any endeavor which Holmes had wrought.

He would deal with Lloyd George in time, but he must find Yardley, if he were still alive, and discover the truth of what had occurred.

When Holmes went about personally examining various and sundry nefarious projects, he always went in the particular disguise of the fictional person he created, Clay's trusted lieutenant, a soullessly efficient Mr. Stash; a rather appropriate name, obviously chosen to evoke, eponymously, exactly that.

To his minions, Clay was still on his journey and no one knew when he would return.

The disguise of Holmes' now ever-increasingly deluded faculties was the same as in New York, but with some additional flourishes. Mr. Stash was a man with full facial hair, russet-brown, a threatening black eye patch over his right eye, and always dressed in a variety of unkempt clothing. He also wielded an oak walking stick, with the head of a werewolf at its tip; which he waved menacingly at any recalcitrant clod.

But Stash had the power and peril of Clay to back him up. So everyone took orders and obeyed without question.

Mr. Stash, indeed.

Tragedy In Eleuthera

It was quite late into the night and Reilly and Tatiana had long ago put baby Sidney to bed.

As usual, they had stood for a long period, just looking down at him. This night, Reilly had said, "He should be lying in a crib fit for a member of the Romanov Royal Family. A rather large crib made of exquisitely carved ebony and inlaid with mother-of-pearl and trimmed at the edges in gold."

"Oh, dear, much too gaudy. And we can't have that now, can we?" said Tatiana playfully. "But Sidney lies asleep every night in a beautiful crib carved from one of the trees that fell during that hurricane. The head gardener, Funny Oscar, my favorite, actually, made it for him. He was here before we even arrived."

"Oh?"

They went into their bedroom, adjoining the nursery and Tatiana continued.

"Yes. Gardeners and house help were here when we arrived. We just assumed they were all from the island, some white, some Negro, and they've taken care of us in a most wonderful way. Especially Funny Oscar. I think he said he was originally from Kent.

"Sidney, sometimes I truly do feel that I'm back at Livadia."

"Funny Oscar... oh, yes. The man who's always smiling, always there to help; and he sleeps in that hammock just outside from time to time, like a guard dog. But I see nothing particularly funny about him. What is it that makes him so funny?" asked Reilly.

136

"Nothing that we can see, either. That's just his name. Funny Oscar."

"Well, it's a funny name to have, if you ask me."

"I don't suppose you were asked, were you?" And she impishly tapped him on the nose with her index finger.

"No, I don't suppose I was." With that, Tatiana closed their bedroom door leading to the hall and they retired for the night.

All the bedrooms were on the second floor. As you came up the stairs, Reilly's and Tatiana's was the first on the right, with baby Sidney's nursery adjoining through a door to the left.

Alexei's room came next on the right with Anastasia's next on the right after that.

Marie's was the first on the left with Olga's next on the left.

The Tsar and Tsarina were at the end of the hallway, straight ahead.

It was about midnight when the door to the solarium, where the Tsarina usually sat, slowly opened. The man who had been watching from outside entered with the silence of a cat. He held a knife in his right hand. Though most lights had been extinguished, night lights had been left on throughout the house, as was usual practice.

He slowly made his way from the solarium to the next room, which was a large open room, with three corridors leading to other rooms, a hallway directly in front to the front doors, and a graceful staircase to the right, leading upstairs. This he proceeded to negotiate with supreme stealth.

It was on the third step that he heard footsteps above, but could not see who was making them. Then, suddenly, a young man's voice yelled out, "Bandit! Thief! Help! Help!"

In an instant, Alexei, totally ignoring the mortal injury he could cause himself, ran down the stairs and threw himself on top of the intruder.

Within only a few moments Reilly was rushing down the stairs, as well. He knew he had to separate Alexei from the intruder and what would happen if he handled Alexei too roughly; but Alexei was already being pummeled. He pulled Alexei away from the man, almost throwing him aside.

Reilly struggled with the man as Funny Oscar, who had heard Alexei screaming
from his hammock, hurried to Reilly's aid. In another moment, it was done. The man was overcome and left on the floor; bound and gagged with large, dirty cloths from Funny Oscar's back pockets. He was then subjected to some severe kicks to the solar plexus and head by Reilly.

Breathing heavily, Reilly managed, "Funny Oscar, thank you."

It was then that the Romanovs came running down the stairs and the Grand Duchesses started screaming. Reilly turned his head to see Alexei bleeding badly. He had been stabbed when he threw himself upon the intruder.

Olga told Funny Oscar to run to the doctor who lived on the grounds; this was the young Royal Navy physician, Ensign Lasker, sent after I had sailed home. He knew nothing of the Romanov's true identity.

Reilly was trying to staunch the blood flowing so violently, giving way to the Tsar attempts, while the rest of those gathered could do nothing but stand about helplessly. All the women were weeping horribly and the Tsar fought tears as he pressed and pressed on the wound, trying to hold Alexei's skin together with his fingers.

"Alexei, Alexei. Don't leave me, Alexei," the Tsar kept saying over and over.

By the time Lasker arrived, it was apparent that Alexei had perished.

I cannot imagine the horror and grief in that house at that instant. But while the Romanovs wept and the physician tried to soothe them, Reilly had other dark matters with which to contend.

With the help of Funny Oscar, Reilly brought the intruder down to the lower level of the house, to a type of storage cellar. This was done out of sight of the physician, so busy was he with Alexei and the family.

The man was sat upright in a wooden straight-backed chair, his arms tied to the back, his feet to the front.

Then Reilly asked Funny Oscar to go back upstairs and help the family in any way possible. He most certainly did not want any witnesses, either.

Reilly took hold of Funny Oscar's arm, looked directly into his eyes and once again said, "Thank you." This was not only a genuine expression of gratitude, but a silent command to never speak of these terrible events. Funny Oscar understood and nodded.

More than anything, Reilly wanted to torture this man, but he wanted answers even more. So Reilly held the knife that had just slain Alexei close to the man's right eye, turned the knife this way then that, and whispered, "You may be of more use to me alive."

The man was nodding "yes" so fast Reilly thought he might haemorrhage.

"I need questions answered. You will give me those answers, yes?"

The man's head continued its radical movement.

"But if you don't answer truthfully, I can assure you that I will cut out your eyes, your balls, slit your throat, shove them all into the hole in your throat, and throw you to the sharks when I'm done."

The man's eyes were as wide as was humanly possible and he had soiled himself, as well.

"I even have a physician upstairs who I'll ask to help you with your wounds. Now, you won't make a sound when I remove the gag. Yes?"

The man was sweating, crying, but the head nods continued unabated.

"All right. We'll try this. But if you utter one sound other than answering the questions I'm about to ask, you know what will happen. Are we understood?"

A single nod this time.

Reilly slowly removed the gag.

"Who are you?"

The man could hardly speak but spat out, in Russian, "Nicholai Enelkin."

"Enelkin, I killed him in Helsinki. How can you be Enelkin?."

Though Reilly spoke in English, the man responded in Russian.

"No, no, you… killed Anatoly Gersikov."

"I don't understand," Reilly said holding the knife to the man's right eye.

"All my men were under orders that if captured or tortured they were to give my name."

"Why?"

"So the others would think I was dead. They would think the head had been cut off, the body would die. I could then go on. If my men didn't do this, their families will be killed. I have been following you since you left Russia. I watched you kill my men. You and the Finn."

"Who sent you?"

"Stalin. He wants you to work for him. He wants to know what you know. He wants to do away with Trotsky. We were to bring you back. If that did not work we were to kill you.

"I never heard of you. The Finn did, though."

"The Patriots. We are the Patriots. We work for Stalin. We do what he wants."

"But you had plenty of chances to kill me. In Finland, England, on the boats. Why didn't you?"

"Once I saw you with the Finn, who I know is SIS, I thought there was more than we knew. I decided to follow you to see where you would lead. And am I crazy, are those people the Romanovs? Lenin said they are dead."

"No, you're not crazy. But you are dead."

With that, Reilly took the dirty cloth that had been used as the gag, wrapped it around Enelkin's throat and proceeded to strangle him, using the knife as a lever to slowly and continuously tighten the cloth. There would be no blood for evidence.

He stood directly in front of Enelkin as he tightened that cloth and said, "I'm standing here as I squeeze the life out of your despicable carcass so I can watch you die the death you deserve. Then I'll feed you to the sharks.

"Oh, look at you; your face is turning as red as the Bolshevik flag."

Yardley

With the funds flowing in to Holmes as the scotch flowed out to Luciano, Holmes was ready to embark on the next phase of his plan to exact his revenge.

However, there had to be an adjustment made. Lloyd George had been ousted as P.M. earlier in the year, so Holmes would not have the personal pleasure of having him toppled and causing his demise, seemingly at his own hand. But he would still have his revenge by making Lloyd George's name anathema to any Englishman. Simultaneously, he would bring about his death. This will be elaborated upon in good order.

He had also, in the time intervening, found that Captain Yardley was not only alive, but at the Admiralty in London. He had men follow him closely and report his routine.

One night, as Yardley stood outside the Admiralty, bidding some of his naval mates goodnight and about to walk home, an old, black limousine stopped at the curb in front of him. Two men jumped from the auto and forced a startled Yardley into the rear. There sat Holmes, but as Mr. Stash.

The men ran to the front, closed the partition tightly and the limousine drove on.

Yardley's first reaction was to scream at this man, demanding to know who he was and what he wanted. But as Yardley examined the man next to him, he thought he knew him. Then, when he thought he recognised him, he was completely befuddled.

"Holmes?"

"Your powers of recognition have not diminished."

Yardley was elated. "Holmes, you have no idea how often I've wondered about you. If you lived or died or where you might be."

Holmes cut him short. "I'm touched by your concern. Now, perhaps, you will tell me what happened to me?"

"Thank heaven you're alive. I gambled and you won."

"I will not ask politely again," and he pointed to the men in the front seat, "what happened to me?"

Yardley was still in the grip of the entwined emotions of shock and elation.

"Holmes, we had orders on that ship that you were not to survive. Under any circumstances you were not be left alive to return to England."

"By whose orders?"

"That I don't know. But right after we boarded, I was handed an encoded wire that said either I, or someone else on the ship, not named, was to dispense with you. I knew I had to protect you. Do you remember the drinks we had together?" Holmes nodded.

"I put a drug in there to make you sleep. I figured that whoever the other person on board was, he had no history with you and he would most certainly do away with you. So I thought the only chance you had was if I drugged you and put inside that lifeboat.

It was night; I knew where watch was and how to avoid them. We were close enough to the American coast and the currents being friendly, I figured they should carry you to shore and you'd survive."

"Go on."

"In the morning I reported a man overboard. We put out some boats to search, but gave up after a few hours and continued on to England."

"You mentioned the lifeboats. Didn't anyone report one missing?"

"Of course. I'm the one who reported it. I had everything figured out.

"The afternoon previous, I reported trouble with the cables holding No. 3 lifeboat and that I would take care of it. When I reported you gone, I also reported that my seamanship had been lacking and that we had lost the lifeboat. I had also expunged the name of our ship from the lifeboat as an added precaution.

"The captain just laughed, said the King could afford another one, but that in retribution, he expected a bottle of the finest brandy in his cabin before his next voyage. I happily complied with the request."

Holmes had been studying Yardley as if Yardley had been on a slide under his microscope. He concluded that this specimen was benign.

"What you're saying, Captain, is that you saved my life."

"Yes! Exactly! And I am so damn happy that I did."

"No more than I, Captain. No more than I."

Holmes knew that Yardley would keep the secret, so there would be no need of caution. Indeed, Holmes now had found someone he could trust completely with his life; as he already had, without even knowing it. And someone who might be called upon if needed again. Holmes also decided to share with Yardley what Reilly had shared with him.

"Lloyd George? The Prime Minister? I just can't believe it," Yardley said, clearly unsettled.

"William," Holmes said, "you have no idea of the duplicity reigning supreme throughout the world. You have your ship, your oath, God Save the King and you're off."

Yardley sat there quietly thinking, then, "If I may ask, why are you in this disguise?"

"You may not."

Holmes dropped him in Piccadilly, held the door open from the inside for one lingering moment, smiled, then closed the door and the auto went on its way as Yardley stood there just shaking his head and waving goodbye.

Holmes knew he would find a way to repay young Yardley. Perhaps it would flow from the immense funds he was accumulating through the sale of spirits to the Americans; and funds from his other, more local, enterprises.

In any event, his financial power would now be used to acquire equivalent political power.

Holmes And Dougie And Mary And Winnie

In our constitutional monarchy, as in any democratic form of government, our elected representatives are not always the altruistic models of rectitude they portray themselves to be. Some are nothing more than hogs at troughs.

It was those particular individuals that Holmes, as Stash, began to cultivate. Some paltry pounds here, some shiny shillings there, and before you knew it, you might have built yourself a very tidy base of politicians who would not only dance to your tune, but would play the music, as well; discordant as it might be.

As Holmes easily learned, it was not just in the House of Commons; indeed no. There were those in the House of Lords who needed substantial financial support even more. Whether to help keep up their large estates, or to continue indulging their tastes of notorious variety; it made no matter.

It was one of those men in the House of Lords who offered to introduce Holmes to another in the House of Lords who might be able to help Holmes further his agenda.

Because he was to meet this high-born personage near Parliament, Holmes felt that Mr. Stash should attire himself appropriately; which he did. He had one of his men drop him off in very close proximity to his destination.

As he walked passed Parliament a bit after noon, thinking about the damage he would do to some inside, he heard a commotion behind and turned to see a huge crowd following two people out of the visitors' entrance by Cromwell Green; two people he knew all too well.

He tried to speed his pace but it was too late as he heard, "Hey, Johnny! John! How the hell are ya?"

Holmes turned to see Fairbanks coming at him full bore with outstretched hand and the other pulling Pickford along like a toy on a string. The crowd ran after them.

"Here, quick, get into our limo," Fairbanks said as a gigantic Rolls-Royce stopped and he pushed Pickford in first, then Holmes, then jumped in and closed the door as he yelled to the driver, "Gun it, pal!"

Holmes had only heard about the ability of a Rolls-Royce of this size to attain such high velocity so quickly; and had it not been for the unfortunate fact of being inside one with Fairbanks and Pickford, the experience would have seemed much more agreeable.

"Hiya, Johnny," slurred Pickford as she kissed Holmes' cheek than reached for the flask inside her purse. "How the hell you been?"

"Boy, oh, boy am I happy to see you," Fairbanks said. "It's been, what, two years? Now I'll be able to show you how I repay a debt. Driver, take us back to our hotel."

"Really, there's no reason for any debt repayment. I was happy to help."

"Nonsense, Johnny, you're gonna have the biggest steak and a bottle of the best champagne in the world with Mary and me."

"No, really, that's totally unnecessary. And I have only recently eaten lunch."

"But we haven't. I'm starved."

"Me, too," Pickford said as she took another sip from a flask that now seemed alarmingly empty. She turned it upside down, shook it and asked, "Who the hell's been drinking my booze?"

"You have, Mary. Only you," Fairbanks said with great frustration; but it seemed to calm her down and she sat quietly till they reached the Savoy; where they had honeymooned.

As usual, Fairbanks helped Pickford from the auto, and Holmes once again tried to free himself from this ridiculous bondage, but to no avail. Fairbanks grabbed Pickford by one elbow, Holmes the other, and pushed them through the doors and then to the sumptuous dining hall; where they were greeted as royalty and shown to their special table.

"Bring us a bottle of your best bubbly," Pickford said, literally licking her lips. Fairbanks ordered "the biggest steaks in England and pronto."

The champagne appeared almost instantaneously; perhaps because they had already anticipated Pickford's penchant for champagne; or any alcohol, for that matter. The sommelier filled their glasses with most a choice champagne, Veuve Cliquot.

"I propose a toast," Fairbanks said, raising his glass, "to friendship."

"Bravo," said Pickford as she downed her first glass before Fairbanks and Holmes had taken their first sip.

"So, John, I guess you're wondering what the hell we're doing back here, huh?"

"The question hadn't crossed my mind."

"Well, we're here for the premiere of my latest picture."

"Doug is just great in it; aren't you, Dougie?" Pickford asked, tousling his hair with her left hand as she sipped her second glass of champagne with her right.

"You bet! And you're never gonna guess who I'm playing," Fairbanks said. "Go ahead, guess, Johnny."

"Marie Antoinette," said Holmes.

After an appropriate double-take from Fairbanks and Pickford spitting her champagne all over the table, Fairbanks started laughing uproariously while Pickford seemed piqued at the waste of a perfectly good glass of champagne. The sommelier refilled her glass.

When Fairbanks stopped laughing and slapping the table, he said, "No, no. I'll give you a hint: the name of the movie is *The Mystery of the Leaping Fish*."

"You're playing Moby Dick," Holmes said.

Another spray of Veuve Cliquot across the table. The same reaction from Fairbanks and Pickford; but this time, she grabbed Holmes' arm and said, "Johnny, would you please not answer again until I've finished drinking my champagne?" The sommelier repeated his task.

"No, John. I play that famous detective of yours over here, that Holmes fella."

This time it was Holmes who gasped, a touch of champagne escaping his mouth and falling on the table.

"Hey, it must be catching," said Pickford, feeling her forehead with the back of her hand to see if she had a fever.

"But how is that possible, Douglas? Did you receive Mr. Holmes' permission?" Holmes asked.

"Didn't need to because we don't use his name. Patent infringement laws. The guy's name in the movie is Coke

Ennyday, get it? And let me tell you, the guy's a real coke addict, poor slob. But the movie is a rip-roaring comedy. You'll piss your pants, it's so funny."

Holmes just sat there in silence. His seven percent solution had, of course, been

chronicled by me, but he was sensitive to his use of the drug and here Fairbanks was telling him that he would be made mockery of the world over. He stood.

"You'll forgive me, but I must really be off."

"What's the matter, John? The steaks aren't even here yet."

"I understand that, but when you kidnapped me, I was on my way to meet with a gentleman who was to give me an introduction to another gentleman I need to speak with about a certain business matter."

"C'mon, sit down. I know everybody who's anybody anyplace. I can introduce you to anyone you want."

Holmes still stood. "Douglas, I cannot offend the man who, I believe, is waiting for me."

"Sure you can. Don't you worry," Fairbanks said as he grabbed Holmes' arm and pulled him back into his seat; just as the steaks were arriving.

"I have a great idea, John. I don't know what kind of business you're in, and I shoulda asked on the ship, but you see that guy at that table over there?" Fairbanks was pointing at a man Holmes knew had once been high in Lloyd George's government. "Is he someone you might want to meet?" Holmes nodded affirmatively.

"Then you just sit here and wait," Fairbanks said and he walked over to the man who rose to greet Fairbanks with a hearty handshake and the taps on the shoulder of friends.

Holmes watched as Fairbanks pointed to him as he spoke to the man. The man looked over, nodded to Holmes, put his cigar down, wrote something on a matchbook and gave it to Fairbanks. The man sat again and Fairbanks returned.

"Here, you're gonna meet him there later; wherever that is. I told you I could introduce you to anyone."

"Thank you, Douglas. Yes, I think your friend might do very nicely, indeed."

The man who Fairbanks had arranged to meet Holme that evening had been the First Lord of the Admiralty in the Great War, was not in a position of any great authority at the moment; but would like to be, once again.

Holmes was to meet him at the Carlton Club, an exclusive club for members of the Conservative Party at 94 Pall Mall; so old that its establishment predated the coronation of Queen Victoria by five years.

The man was Winston Churchill.

A grandson of the 7th Duke of Marlborough; yet he had no title of nobility; a very perplexing political mixture.

Churchill was already financially comfortable, so he could not be bribed. His intellect was of the first order so he could not be duped. He loved his wife and five children so he could not be blackmailed. But as with any politician, he was not above a harmless quid pro quo. And Holmes believed he had such an exchange that Churchill would easily accept.

"Sir Winston," Holmes began, as he and Churchill raised a whiskey towards each other, "I have heard so many good things about you from our mutual acquaintances."

"Quite," said Churchill briskly as he took another puff of his ubiquitous cigar. "And I have inquired about you and have heard some interesting things, myself, Mr. Clay or Mr. Stash or whomever you may choose to call yourself."

Holmes had been forewarned that this man was not one who appreciated idle banter or casual social pleasantries; unless he was the instigator of them. And he had just proven his connections to unnamed investigative authorities.

"Then I shall get right to point," said Holmes. "I believe that you might enjoy an important post within Mr. Baldwin's government." Stanley Baldwin was our new P.M.

"That is no secret, sir. If you have anything to put to me, please do so," and he took another sip of whiskey.

"At once. You see, it seems that one of Mr. Baldwin's most trusted political allies, a man of the highest aristocracy, but of basest tastes, is about to be appointed to a rather senior position within the cabinet, the Chancellor of the Exchequer."

Holmes saw that he now had the fullest attention of Churchill. He continued.

"This man had been having certain fetishes catered to by one of his herdsman, a man who shared like interests." Churchill leaned in towards Holmes, he loved political gossip; the more vile, the better.

"Mr. Baldwin would be made aware that should he not appoint you to this position instead of the aforementioned individual, well, then who's to tell how certain stories may suddenly appear in the Sunday Times..." Holmes leaned back in his chair and shrugged his shoulders.

"I see, Mr. Clay, I most certainly do see," Chruchill said as he sipped his whiskey, took another puff and likewise leaned back; this time with a satisfied grin. After a meditative moment he spoke again. "And just what, Mr. Clay, might be expected from a Chancellor?"

"This is a post from which one so high can see so much going on below; if he's looking in the right direction. Or not see something if he might be looking in another."

"Am I to understand that the Chancellor might be given a nod in which direction to look or not, and when?"

"That might be expected, yes."

"Of course, it would have to be noted that the Chancellor would never look, or not look, in a particular direction if he thought it would, in any way, harm Great Britain, the Empire or any of its people," Churchill said firmly. "There would be no underpinnings of the underworld. That should be thoroughly understood."

"That would be most certainly noted," replied Holmes.

"Then, I believe, Mr. Baldwin should be expecting some much unexpected news shortly?" Churchill asked.

"I do believe so," Holmes replied.

The men clinked glasses. And Holmes noticed that the smoke streaming from Churchill's cigar was encircling his head like a halo.

The Grand Duchesses Disperse

Reilly had left Enelkin's body in the corner of that storage room and had gone back to Tatiana and the family to console them as much as possible. But also, and to him, of paramount importance, to command each to say nothing of the man who had killed Alexei. Reilly would speak with Lasker about cause of death.

The next night, thankfully, shed enough light for him to see. As the Romanovs slept, he went back downstairs, shoved the body into a burlap sack and labouriously pulled the body up, then across the lawn to the dock. He then kicked the body into a rowboat.

Funny Oscar watched silently from under a palm tree.

Large rocks were stuffed in the sack, Reilly carrying each, one by one because of their weight. He then tied the sack shut and rowed out a fair enough distance which he judged to be sufficiently far enough that the chances of discovery would be minimal.

Enelkin was then thrown overboard and Reilly rowed back, Enelkin sinking quickly.

Lasker did what he was empowered to do, and pronounced Alexei dead due to his hemophilia on February 12, 1922; two days after his actual death. He would deal with the local officials so there would be no disturbing inquiries.

He had also attended to the Romanov's understandable hysteria and administered sedatives to all, except the Tsarina, who had slept through the turmoil and did not seem aware of the sadness surrounding her, nor of anything else, for that matter.

While the family grieved inconsolably, it was Anastasia, the closest in age to Alexei who took it most severely. The fun-loving, irrepressible girl had suddenly begun to become, like her mother, withdrawn, quiet, and morose. Perhaps she was still in shock, Lasker thought, and did everything he could to bring her around; but was without success.

Since there were no Russian Orthodox clergy on the island, it was agreed that the doctor, since he represented His Majesty's government, even so tenuously, would officiate at Alexei's funeral.

It was further agreed that the burial site would be on the compound, but would remain unmarked. It would be left to nature to provide the cover for Alexei's final resting place. Only the family would attend, and Funny Oscar; because the night before the service, it was he who dug Alexei's grave at the spot selected and wept no less than the Romanovs.

"Emerald green grass and beautiful wild flowers will keep him even warmer in the Eleutheran sun," said Anastasia, aloud.

The Tsar was inconsolable. Besides losing his only beloved son, he also knew that his direct Romanov line had just been truly extinguished. Should there be a restoration of his rule, however unlikely that may be, the throne would pass to his brother, Michael, and not to any of his issue. Even baby Sidney could not be considered because Reilly was a commoner. But those thoughts were kept to himself and only intuited by Reilly.

If the burden of Alexei's death were not enough, Lasker was grieved to report to the family that, "The Tsarina has slipped so far into her world that she has completely left ours." And within the week, the Tsarina passed, too. Perhaps into the world she had already inhabited for the longest time.

"I have lost the essence of my essence. My Sonny has gone to be with Alexei," said the Tsar. The Tsarina was laid to rest beside Alexei.

Tatiana, of course, had Reilly and baby Sidney for love and consolation, but with the other Grand Duchesses, it was a final ephemeral bond severed.

After a proper time of grieving as prescribed by their faith, Tatiana, Marie, Olga and Anastasia gathered to discuss what they would do now. They were all young women, vibrant, intelligent and now free to explore the world from which they had been so long sequestered.

Olga was twenty-five, Marie was twenty-one and Anastasia was only nineteen.

It was agreed that Tatiana would remain on Eleuthera with the Tsar so that he would have, at least, one loving daughter to look after him; and baby Sidney would be there, as well, of course. The other Grand Duchesses were to lead lives of their own.

They had long before been supplied with new identities and British passports, so there would be no trouble in their emigration from the island. There would also be no trouble in securing the finances needed to establish new lives, since the Romanovs had established healthy secret accounts in Switzerland which could now be reclaimed. These would be more than sufficient to begin their new lives anywhere in the world they would so choose.

After much introspection and debate, they decided to travel to disparate destinations. Olga would be going to the United States, to New York. Marie and Anastasia would be going to England, to London.

These were mammoth cities within which one would easily lose oneself. And because each spoke English fluently with a proper, upper-class British accent, through years of tutorials by proper British tutors, it would be quite easy for Marie and Anastasia to blend in, in London. For Olga in New York, her accent would only enhance her appeal.

It's a rather likeable trait of the Americans to believe that anyone with a British accent is more intelligent, more refined, more cultured, and, in every way, superior to them. Which, while not necessarily true in every instance, is, overall, a correct attitude for them to have.

In addition, Reilly could not stress one point more forcefully to Marie and Anastasia: while they would reside in London, no matter how strong the desire, no contact was to be made with me to insure my safety and that of my family. To this, both agreed most wholeheartedly. Neither would want to bring harm to me or my family.

To keep security to a maximum, they turned to Reilly. As difficult as this would be for them to accept, but to insure the success and safety of their new lives, he alone would make all arrangements. He would leave the island to make these arrangements in Nassau and for the time being, he alone would know where each would reside.

At the start, each would have a temporary residence in which to live and from which they would explore their new city and decide on a permanent residence; which would be purchased for them with the Romanov funds.

Then, when each of the Grand Duchesses had established their new residences and deemed it a safe interval, they would post their addresses, in a code devised by Reilly, to Tatiana, who would then send them on to the others. No one outside of the family would know anything of their new identities or destinations. No one.

Reilly also cautioned them that contact between them should only be made because of a most dire development. Their very lives depended on their complete circumspection.

Once again, Reilly called on Funny Oscar to help with the packing, indeed, for all preparations for the Grand Duchesses' departures; which he did with great sadness. The Grand Duchesses had become as family to him. He had lost Alexei, the Tsarina, and now these young ladies who had been so gracious and kind to him and those who worked with him at Winding Bay.

It was further decided that each would leave individually, at intervals of two weeks, to reduce any ambient suspicion of the ladies' departures. Olga would leave first, then Marie, then, finally, Anastasia; who at last was, if not herself, at least somewhat out of the depression in which she had been since Alexei's death.

And, as with all children leaving their parents' care to make their way in the world, they experienced the seemingly incompatible emotions of exuberant exhilaration and dreadful trepidation. But even Grand Duchesses are human, after all.

The family gathered at their small dock to say goodbye to Olga; with full knowledge that they may never see her again.

All the Grand Duchesses tearfully embraced and whispered words of love and assurance, Olga taking extra time in kissing baby Sidney, then they gave way to the Tsar, who was weeping copiously because another piece of his being was being sundered.

"I shall never see you again, Olga, my first born."

"Yes, you shall, Papa, you shall."

But not wanting to prolong this tender agony, Olga turned and went into the boat, Reilly holding her hand from the deck as he helped her on board the little skiff which would take them to Nassau; and from there, she would begin her voyage to New York.

The little skiff left immediately, Olga waving a handkerchief, the remaining ladies doing likewise, and the Tsar simply waving dispiritedly. In a very few moments, the skiff was out of sight and the family returned to the main house.

This same sadness was repeated for Marie and then, finally for Anastasia. Unlike her sisters, though also terribly disheartened by the family's separation, she exhibited an unconcealed ennui at beginning her new life. And then, she, too, was gone.

When Reilly had returned to Tatiana after seeing Anastasia off safely to England from Nassau, he looked especially pensive.

"Yes," Tatiana said, "I know. This must all weigh on you so."

"Tatiana, I can't escape the unrelenting thought that had I hadn't come here, none of this would've happened."

"My darling, please, please don't blame yourself. It was only natural for you to want to be with me and Sidney. You would've been a monster not to have. We can't say what would've, or wouldn't have happened if you hadn't come."

"I know, I know, but that doesn't change what I feel."

Tatiana then embraced Reilly and held him as if all his turmoil and travail would leave him and be transferred to her.

But Reilly knew that if all I had told him were so, then Lloyd George and the others involved were responsible for these tragic events on the island. The deaths of Alexei and the Tsarina and the diaspora of the Romanovs were to be laid directly at their feet. But ultimately, Lloyd George.

He would wait a sufficient time to be sure all was secure and safe on the island for Tatiana, baby Sidney and the Tsar; but then he would return to London and exact his own vengeance.

What he could not know or imagine, was that his desire for revenge would place

him on a lethal collision course with Holmes. Reilly would be intent on taking his revenge on Lloyd George; but, in a truly bizarre twist, Holmes would be even more intent on preventing that from happening.

Now Or Never

More than two years had passed since Holmes had returned to London and he was adding and subtracting elements of his revenge like an abacus gone awry.

On the plus side, Holmes had a criminal underworld at his command. Also on the plus side, Churchill was still Chancellor of the Exchequer. However, on the minus side, Churchill was foundering as Chancellor.

Perhaps most portentous, Holmes had not discovered any enchanted elixir of youth; he was getting on.

Ultimately, however, with Lloyd George no longer Prime Minister, Holmes could take his revenge; and in a way in which Lloyd George would be discredited to the world.

To Holmes, it seemed a perfect plan. But as he himself, once said, "Any time anyone announces he has devised a perfect plan, I immediately assume him to be a perfect fool."

All that was left was his private confrontation with Lloyd George. It was time for Churchill to look in a set direction and arrange a meeting. Churchill would know nothing of its true import.

However, not even Holmes could imagine its ultimate outcome.

A New Yorker In London

It was at this time that a certain man arrived in London. A man using London as a stop on the way to a place of extreme importance to the continued success of his and his partners' business. A man who first, however, had to visit his British business partner, Clay. But Holmes had no prior knowledge that this man was coming. The man and his partners had wanted it that way. The man was Bugsy Siegel.

Holmes was immediately made aware of his presence by those he paid to inform him of such consequential matters. Siegel had checked into one of the newest and poshest hotels in London, an Art Deco delight, the Cumberland. So innovatively modern was this hotel, that it was the first in London to offer direct dial telephones and to have bathrooms in each suite.

The morning after arriving in London, Siegel tried to have breakfast in the Centre Court. I will explain the "why" in a moment, then had the front man hail a cab for him and got in.

"Yeah, buddy, I wanna go to Varrance Road and Lomas Street. You know where this place is?"

The driver turned to look at Siegel. "I should certainly hope so," said the driver. It was Holmes. But his disguise as Mr. Stash was the same he had used as John Clay, but without the eye patch, so nothing seemed strange to Siegel.

Siegel laughed heartily and said, "Ya know, Meyer told me that even though we didn't tell you I was coming, I wouldn't find you first; that you'd find me. Damn Meyer, he's always right." And he continued to laugh as Holmes began to drive to his headquarters.

"Hey, Johnny, you people here in England don't speak English."

"Why is that, Ben?"

"Okay, so I go down to have breakfast at that Centre Court; real fancy. The waiter brings over a menu and right away I know I'm in trouble."

"I don't understand," Holmes said.

"You don't understand? It was like they handed me a menu in Greek.

"I take a gander at the menu; the first thing I see is crumpets. I look up at the waiter and ask him 'what the hell is a crumpet?' He says it's like an English muffin. So I say 'why the hell don't you say so?'

"Then I take a look and there's bangers and mash. Now I'm really gettin' frustrated. To me it sounds like a gat and a club you smash someone over the head with. So I say, 'What the hell is this? Some kinda weapon or somethin'?' He explains they're sausage and mashed potatoes.

"Now, here's the topper. I take a look at the menu again and I think somebody spelled this thing wrong. It says kippers; and I'm thinkin' zippers. So I ask the guy again, 'What the hell is a kipper?' And he says it's a fish. And I get excited.

"You got gefilte fish? I ask the guy. He looks at me like I'm nuts.

"He says, 'I beg your pardon.'

"Don't go beggin' my pardon, buddy; ya go to the governor for that. Just bring me some eggs, bacon and one of them crumpets. I coulda starved before I got any food."

"Well I'm sure you didn't come for our gastronomical delights or sightseeing, Ben. Why don't you tell me why London is graced with your splendid, sartorial presence?"

"Sure thing, Johnny. Not that Lucky and Meyer and me don't trust you…"

"Perish the thought."

"Yeah, well things are gettin' tight back in New York. We got guys tryin' to muscle in on our territory and they're spreading word around that they're buyin' their booze from you. I'm here to see if it's true."

"And if it is," Holmes asked, "you're to 'rub me out', correct?"

"Yeah, that's about it," Siegel said as he examined his manicure.

Now it was Holmes who laughed. Slightly.

Holmes had seen Siegel's savagery first hand during the Castellammarese War. He had a very unsavory taste of why Siegel was called Bugsy; but never called that to his face. And now Holmes knew how completely mad Siegel must have been to come three thousand miles into Holmes' territory without an ally, to try to kill him and still come out alive.

But of course, that was it: Siegel never thought otherwise. To Siegel, the thought of his own mortality never entered what there was of his mind. He never even gave the thought of failure a thought.

Holmes assured Siegel that he and Lansky and Luciano had nothing to worry about. If it's one virtue he held above all others, it was loyalty.

"Yeah," Siegel said, "that's what Benedict Arnold told George Washington." Now Holmes really laughed. And they drove on.

Reilly Leaves Eleuthera

It was time for Reilly to return to London. It was now May, all was safe and secure on Eleuthera and as much as he wanted to remain, he felt he could leave, accomplish this one last mission, and return to the love of his family for good.

Tatiana was, of course, distraught.

"But why must you go, Sidney? What wrenches you from us? What is so important?"

"Tatiana, you know me. You know me better than any living being. And because you know me, you know that there's something I must do or betray all in me you love. Please don't ask me not to go because I can't deny you anything. But I promise you that I'll return as soon as possible. I wouldn't want to waste one moment."

Tatiana paused, holding back tears.

"Then I won't ask you to stay, but how long do you think you'll be gone?"

"Months, I think."

"Months? Oh, Sidney…"

Reilly took her in his arms. He knew he had just won this gentle battle.; but the one to come would not be so easy. He made ready.

The next day, the Tsar accompanied Reilly, who held little Sidney, and Tatiana to the dock. Funny Oscar was there, as he always was when family was leaving. Little Sidney was crying.

"No, no, don't cry, Sidney. Daddy is just going on an adventure and will be back very soon," Reilly said, kissing him as he spoke.

"No, daddy, no daddy. Don't go, daddy."

It was breaking all their hearts and Tatiana, always so sensitive to these things,
took little Sidney from Reilly, held him in her arms close to her bosom and rocked comfortingly back and forth, consoling him.

Reilly gave Tatiana one last kiss, and as he stepped into the skiff, Funny Oscar came forward to shake hands. As they did so, Reilly felt a small slip of paper being placed surreptitiously in his hand. He didn't react but saw Funny Oscar smiling warmly and giving him a knowing wink. Reilly thought to himself, "Now, what was that all about?"

In a few minutes the skiff was out of sight and Reilly, done waving at his family, turned to unfold and examine the paper that Funny Oscar had given him.

He smiled and had the answer to the question he had just asked.

Reilly kept that paper, carrying it as a good luck talisman for his entire life, I believe. The last time he visited me, he showed me that little scrap of paper. I shall now try to duplicate, in my meager manner, the three simple letters that were on it: S ‡ S

Funny Oscar

So, Funny Oscar was SIS.

All Reilly could do was wonder what had brought Funny Oscar to Eleuthera and how he had gotten that name. As Funny Oscar told him much later, this is what brought him there.

At the beginning of the Great War, the Germans began trying to foment trouble in as many of the British Caribbean islands as possible. They had sent agents to incite the local Negro populations against the white colonials. However, the Germans had not met with any success.

The Admiralty had sent a handful of SIS operatives to combat the Germans and Funny Oscar wound up in Eleuthera where, it was reported, a German U-boat had been frequently seen and its sailors and officers had come ashore to stir up the locals.

In a way, that wass absolutely true. And in another, perhaps not.

It was the U-24. It had surfaced three times at the southernmost tip of Eleuthera near Bannerman Town. On each of those times, a contingent of officers and sailors had stolen ashore. However, the contingent was comprised of different men each time.

The officers and sailors of the U-24, it seemed, just couldn't take the claustrophobic feeling of their vessel anymore, needed some female companionship and were more than willing to seek it with the native women; who, in turn, were happy for the silver coins they received.

What happened next gave Funny Oscar his name.

Oscar and the local constabulary had already learned of the Germans' tete-a-tetes from one of the women who walked into their station and said "I am loyal to King George and those Germans smell bad."

So Oscar planned a little surprise for the Germans.

First, all the women being visited were brought into the police station. Oscar, backed up by some constables, spoke to the women and reminded them that they were subjects of the Crown and that what they were doing was collaborating with the enemy. They could be taken out and shot for that.

Well, you can imagine the commotion, the crying, and the piteous beseeching to spare them.

"Of course," Oscar said, calming them down. "Not only will you be spared, but I'll give you all the chance to become national heroes."

At this, the commotion and crying and piteous beseeching ceased and the women started happy yells and dancing around. Finally, one of them asked, "How?"

"It's quite simple," Oscar said. "This is what I want you to do."

They knew that the Germans were due to return the next night. So as the officers and sailors of U-24 were busily engaged in visiting these women, their uniforms were being whisked away by other women who were not visiting.

When the Germans were through, they discovered that their uniforms had vanished.

Well, you can imagine the commotion, the screaming the searching for their uniforms as they ran about as natural as the day they were born.

It was at this precise moment that Oscar and the constables arrested all of the Germans who were then forced to march through Bannerman Town as the locals laughed and jeered and mocked them and threw fruits and vegetables, as well.

The sergeant in command of the constables kept repeating, as he laughed, "That is so funny, Oscar. That is so funny, Oscar."

And so, to the locals and everyone else, Oscar became Funny Oscar ever after.

Where The Doves Had Flown

Upon her arrival in England, Marie, now Mary Hampton, moved into a home already purchased by the Romanovs in the late nineteenth century, but held in trust through well-retained solicitors in Zurich.

The home was at 23 Chester Square in Belgravia, one of London's most prestigious addresses; and directly next to where Mary Shelley, the author of "Frankenstein", once lived. Odd coincidence, that.

Marie fell in love with the house and decided to make that her permanent residence.

Anastasia, now Anna Anders, chose to live in a community more alive with the artistic and intellectual life blossoming in London right after the war; best likened to Greenwich Village in New York City. She chose to live in Bloomsbury, at No. 2
Theobald's Road.

It had a lovely garden and was quite private. She had once remarked to Marie that when she tended to her garden, her garden tended to her. A sentiment anyone in England could easily embrace.

Though each lived not far from each other, they infrequently met and Marie saw how deeply Anastasia still grieved for her lost brother, retreating further into her own secluded world.

On a more happy note, while Marie was strolling through Grosvenor Square only   a few months after arriving, a hand fell gently on her shoulder and startled her. As she turned to see who it was, she gasped. It was William Yardley. Had he not held her upright, she would have fainted onto the pavement. William led her to a bench where he sat her down and held her hands, assuring her that he was not a mirage.

"William, I thought you were dead. I heard your ship had been sunk." She was about to tell all that Reilly had told her and her on Eleuthera when she remembered his directive to not disclose any of what he had told them. She thought it best to ask him questions.

"What happened to you? What about your ship sinking? And what about Mr. Holmes?"

William, happy though uncomfortable, said, "Well, you can see that I'm here, holding your beautiful hands, so I guess I'm still alive."

"Now stop that," she said, playfully admonishing him, "you've given me quite a shock, you know. I might have had a heart attack, and then where would you be?"

It was his turn to play act. "I would have perished right alongside you for causing the death of the woman I love." As those words danced out, he suddenly realized he had spoken the truth and once again became serious and silent. Marie, too, became silent as she looked into his eyes.

"It's still true, William?"

"Yes…yes."

"Then why didn't you contact me to let me know you were alive? Why let me think you were dead all this time?"

"Marie, I couldn't. There's much I can't discuss, but as you see from my uniform, I'm still a serving officer in the Royal Navy and I'm bound by honour to follow orders."

"And those orders included not telling me anything? Letting me grieve for you?"

"Those orders forbade me from telling anyone what we all had been through. I have not uttered your name once since leaving you. No, that's a lie. I've spoken your name countless times; but only to myself.

"I reported back to my superiors upon my return, reunited with my father, who had also believed me dead, and resumed by duties. And now, here we are. Please, please forgive me, but any attempt of mine to contact you in any way, shape or form may have endangered you and your family. And though it'll sound trite, I put your safety above my desire to be with you."

"But what of your ship being sunk and what happened to Mr. Holmes?"

"Again, I can't discuss any of that. But please, Marie, just accept that we're together again and make me this promise: that you'll never ask me about these things again."

After a long moment, and with her head downwards, Marie said, "Done."

She then told William of the secrets she could share safely at this time; of her new identity and that Anastasia was there in London, as well. But when pressed for further news of her family, she answered him as he had her.

"As with you, William, there are certain matters I can't speak about; at least not at this time. Therefore, please, as you've asked me, please don't ask me of these matters again. But from now on, please call me, Mary. I know you'll do as I ask because it is important. My name now is Mary Hampton."

As with her answer to him, William replied, "Done."

They continued to sit on that bench, taking simple pleasure in the other's mere presence.

Lucky And Meyer And Bugsy

"Nice place ya got here, Johnny," Siegel said as he stepped from the cab, looking up at the building housing Holmes' headquarters and glancing around at the neighbouring structures. "Nice neighbourhood, too."

"It suffices. Please, follow me upstairs."

Inside the doorway were a number of the most menacing-looking of Holmes' men. Siegel immediately reached for the pistol in his overcoat pocket. The men recoiled.

"Ben, Ben, there's no need for that. These are my men and they carry no firearms. No need. In England there's an unwritten agreement between the constabulary and the criminals: we don't carry weapons and they don't carry weapons."

"What kind a nutty country is this, anyway? Who ever heard of goin' around without a gun?"

"Puzzling, isn't it?." Holmes continued up the stairs as Siegel followed, still intermittently glancing back at the cluster of thugs remaining below.

"A libation?" asked Holmes.

"I thought you'd never ask," Siegel said, looking around, walking around, and before seating at a table, dusting the chair and the table with a very expensive silk handkerchief which he removed from his breast pocket with an outrageously ostentatious gesture.

"Like I said downstairs, nice place ya got here. Johnny, I know you can afford better."

"Yes, but I like it here. It's quiet. Out of the way of prying eyes. With only my eyes allowed to pry."

"L'chaim, Johnny," Siegel said as he raised his glass to Holmes, who wasn't partaking. "Hey, was I nuts or did I see synagogues on the way here?"

"Quite discerning. Yes, at one point, this area was home to a very large portion of members of your faith, mostly from Poland and Eastern Europe."

"Holy mackerel. Just like New York."

"Yes; in fact, most precisely like New York. Funny, I had not made the analogy previously," Holmes said, pondering his omission.

"Well, everyone forgets from time to time. Now lemme see the books," Siegel said with a mild touch of menace.

"Of course. And I presume you will trust my scribbling?" asked Holmes.

Siegel shrugged, "Who the hell knows?"

From a large, locked wooden chest, something that looked like a pirate's chest to Siegel, Holmes proceeded to disgorge large, brown accountancy ledgers; each with its own private lock. These he placed before Siegel who was laughing loudly.

"Ben, if I might inquire, just why are you laughing?"

"Johnny, I'm not sure if you'll get it, but I can tell Meyer and Charlie that you served me locks. Get it?"

Holmes stared blankly.

"Johnny, in New York, remember we used to eat bagels and cream cheese and lox?"

Then it came to Holmes; Siegel had just made a pun based upon an ethnic delicacy.

"Very good, Ben, very good. Perhaps you'd like to peruse the numbers now?"

Siegel finally stopped laughing and began his inspection.

After long and close examination of the ledgers presented and placated, after incisive questioning of Holmes that there were no other records being hidden from his perusal, Siegel was satisfied that Holmes was "on the up and up".

Holmes had watched Siegel intently as he examined the records and was surprised to observe a man of high intelligence and subtle financial acumen; not just the wisecracking mobster he appeared to be.

"Benjamin, you've impressed me."

"Yeah? How come?"

"You appear to be quite well versed with income and expenditure columns and the veiled intricacies of creative accounting. I'm pleased."

"Yeah, well ya should be. I'd have had t' bump you off if you were finagling the books."

"Yes, you already informed me."

"But I'm nothin' compared to Meyer. He's the real brain. Ever since we were little kids; and I mean little. He was already figurin' the odds on craps in back alleys on the lower east side when he was eight. The guy's a real genius."

"I suspected as much from our dealings in New York. And what about Charlie?"

"Charlie leaves the money stuff to Meyer. Not that Charlie don't got it in him. He does. Real good. And trust me, Johnny, Charlie will know if you're tryin' t' pull a fast one. But Charlie's more like the head of the company. Like the dagos call it, capo di tutto capi; the boss of all bosses. Yeah,

Charlie gives the final okays. But he don't do nothin' without Meyer and him talkin' and agreein'."

"They're like brothers, from what I could gather."

"Tighter. Let me tell you somethin'. Meyer is like my older brother. I love that guy like my own flesh and blood. I would do anythin' for Meyer. But him and Charlie got somethin' special. I don't know how t' put it exactly but they're so close that Charlie could begin talkin' and Meyer could finish what he was gonna say. And vice versa."

"Truly exceptional. But can you answer something that I should have asked in New York?"

"Depends on what it is," Siegel said.

"This alliance you have, the Jews and Italians. We have nothing like that here. I would have expected that you would have been at each other's throats."

"Yeah, we were once. We all came over about the same time and moved into the same streets in downtown Manhattan and in Brooklyn. So we started fighting for territory and we had the mick gangs to fight, too.

"Funny, you would think the Catliks would fight together against the Jews, but maybe it's because of tight family, I don't know, but it seemed like the Jews and dagos were fightin' the micks together."

"Extraordinary."

"Yeah, but the clincher was when Meyer saved Charlie's life when they was kids."

"Please tell me what happened."

"Well, it goes back to when Meyer was maybe eight and Charlie was twelve and Charlie already had a gang he was leadin'. So late on Friday afternoon, here comes this little runt Jewish kid. And the kid has his challah money, a nickel."

Holmes interrupted, "I beg your pardon?"

"Challah money," Siegel said, as though everyone in the world with half a brain knew what it meant. "Jews can't cook or bake or do anythin' on Saturday because that's our day of rest the Bible said, or somethin' like that. So the moms would give the kids money to go to the baker on Friday and bring back the challah, the bread, because the moms couldn't bake on Saturday."

"Oh, I see. But why didn't the mothers just bake the bread on Friday themselves and save the money?"

"How the hell do I know? Do I look like a Jewish mother?"

"No, most certainly not," Holmes said.

"So anyway, Charlie tells his gang to stop this little kike and get the money. So they stop Meyer and tell him to hand over the dough. So what does Meyer do? He's holdin' that nickel tight in his skinny little hand and he tells the dagos to go screw 'emselves. But he didn't use such a nice word. Well, they start beatin' on Meyer but as small and skinny as Meyer was, he's givin' as good as he's gettin'.

"Now, Charlie is watchin' all this and he sees that this kid is somethin' else, so he calls off his gang and goes over to Meyer who's bleedin' and banged up, but he's still holdin' on t' that nickel.

"Charlie looks Meyer up and down and kind of smiles and tells him to beat it and not to come through his street again. Meyer gives Charlie the same look up and down and tells him to go screw himself and walks away. But Meyer is smart enough to know that this dago kid just did him a solid and he won't forget.

"Now a couple a weeks go by and Charlie is without his gang and he's swimmin' in the East River. Some mick guys swimmin' there see Charlie and they swim over and are tryin' to drown him when like outta nowhere Charlie feels the micks lettin' go and he fights his way to the top and sees that Meyer is fightin' off the micks.

"So now it's Charlie and Meyer givin' the micks the business. So the micks swim off, Charlie and Meyer are kickin' water in the East River and Meyer is smilin' back at Charlie like 'Were even, pal.' And that's how the whole thing got started."

"Ben, if it came from anyone else but you, I simply would not believe it."

"Yeah, well you can take that to the races. Now I gotta send a wire to let Charlie and Meyer to let them know that I ain't killed ya and the booze is gonna keep comin' t' nobody but us. Then I'm gonna take a few days before I go back t' New York and see if I can meet the King, and see where those dames got their heads cut off. Real culture stuff."

"Yes, you really must."

"And I gotta get me some girls. This town is swimmin' in babes and all are willin' to go dancin', if ya know what I mean."

"Yes, there is a surfeit of young and willing women. The result of the loss of so many of our young and willing men in the Great War."

"Oh, yeah, I got ya. Sorry about that, Johnny. Anyway, I'm scrammin' Don't take any wooden nickels."

As Siegel walked down those stairs, he stopped at the bottom, where those same men were still standing. He looked up at Holmes.

"Hey, how am I gettin' back t' the hotel."

"No worries; one of my men will bring you back in that same cab."

"Ya think he can take me t' where you limeys did all that head cuttin' off stuff?"

"I'm sure it can be arranged." Holmes looked down at one of his men, "Andrew, drive Mr. Siegel to the Tower of London."

The man tipped his right index finger to his cap to indicate "okay" and Siegel followed Andrew out to the cab. As he got in the back with Andrew at the wheel in front, Siegel said, "Hey, pal; how the hell do you guys drive cockeyed like that?"

Andrew shrugged, didn't answer and began the drive to the Tower.

Holmes And Lloyd George And Reilly And Bugsy

The forces of fate were converging. Churchill had set up the clandestine meeting for Holmes at an absent friend's magnificent home in Belgravia, right on Belgrave Square. There, Holmes would surprise Lloyd George.

Holmes had no disguise this night, other than his real facial hair and a hat pulled down as low as possible with the collar of a great overcoat pulled up as high as possible. Only his eyes showed through. He had also removed the patch. Andrew had dropped Holmes off a few houses down and waited for Holmes to return.

Holmes was greeted by the butler who showed him into a lavish library where Lloyd George stood facing a bookcase in the opposite direction of the door. The butler closed the door behind him.

"Prime Minister," Holmes said with a hiss more than a voice.

As Lloyd George turned to face the voice, Holmes was slowly removing his hat and overcoat, tossing them onto a chair.

At first, Lloyd George was frozen, not recognizing the man before him.

"Come, come Prime Minister. After all we've been to each other?"

Then, "Holmes! But you're dead."

"I think not. But you shall soon be."

"This is impossible. I was assured of your death."

"Which proves, I surmise, that we cannot trust anyone. Isn't that true Prime Minister?"

"This is preposterous," Lloyd George said, in a state of disbelief, outrage and vulnerability.

"Preposterous that I live or preposterous that you are caught, trapped. But have no fear, I shan't harm you now. What I have planned for you is much more subtle and fitting."

Lloyd George was trying to move towards the door but Holmes stood blocking it.

"What do you mean?" Lloyd George asked.

Holmes then slowly and maliciously told him about his plan to release the proof of his perfidy and the logical assumption of the events which would follow, subsequently.

"You're mad, Holmes, completely mad. I had nothing to do with ordering your death. Nothing. The orders given were not given by me."

"Not that I would believe you in any manner, but by who then?"

"If you recall that night at 10 Downing, the man you met secretly in a private room?"

"The King?"

"The same. Shortly after you left, I knocked and went into that room. He stood there at that fireplace and bade me sit. The King was not known for his intimacy with those beneath him, even with his P.M.s., so I was gratified, yet mystified, at what further he wished to discuss.

"What concerned me almost immediately was a phrase he used, saying it to himself as I sat."

"Which was?" Holmes asked.

"He said, 'The comedy has begun'. But it was said cryptically; as if it had layered meaning. And based upon subsequent information I received towards the end of the war, I understood that meaning."

"Which was?" Holmes asked again.

"That he expected the rescue to fail."

Holmes stood up straight in disbelief. "What fiendish lie is this?"

"It is no lie, Holmes. Remember, when I mentioned invisible others to you at our meeting? Well, that is precisely what the King wished to impart; however he did not use that term.

"He was not so blind that he did not see that others of very high noble rank or immense wealth had agendas that differed violently from his and my government's. Yet those agendas remained obscure to him, as well as to me.

"To this moment, I still do not know who ordered your death. And I also have no idea who was responsible for the false news to be released about that death. My own quiet inquiries within my special branches produced nothing to refute the verity of your death.

"Holmes, I don't know what you think you are going to do to me, but mark this and mark this carefully: if anything lethal should happen to me, if I took my life by my own hand, or was bitten to death by the Archbishop of Canterbury, Watson would summarily be dispensed with. This was an order I was forced to give to keep secret all I have just recounted.

"And that order is still in force even though I'm no longer Prime Minister. I could give an arcane order at any time to have the deed done; and that would certainly follow any attempt by you at blackmail.

"So, yes, Mr. Holmes, even though I would be disgraced, Watson would be dead."

In essence, I had become Lloyd George's insurance policy.

Holmes had now been forced to become the guarantor of my and Lloyd George's life. And, for the first time, Holmes felt outdone. Not only because he could not move against Lloyd George as he wished, but because based upon what Holmes and the others had experienced in Russia, he could not tell if what Lloyd George had just told him was more fiction or truth.

In any event, Holmes' next utterance was chillingly blasphemous and, to Lloyd George, bordering on the mad.

Holmes said, "I shall shred this table of lies to learn the truth. God, as devil incarnate, has devised more than one way to blot out the sun."

With that, Lloyd George removed a revolver from his case and pointed it at Holmes, gesturing for him to move away from the door. Holmes moved, but only slightly.

Lloyd George then called out to the butler. He called out again. But the butler didn't come.

Holmes And Reilly And Bugsy

Once back in London, it was simple for Reilly to re-establish contact with those at SIS he knew he could trust, and from them, learn Lloyd George's routine. It was public knowledge where he lived, and after that, anyone with a modicum of intelligence could follow his movements. This, Reilly did assiduously. And that is precisely how Reilly followed Lloyd George to that house in Belgravia.

He was willing to wait for Lloyd George to re-emerge from that house and continue to follow. Then he saw an auto stop a few houses away, he watched a man walk to that house and go in; a man bundled so as not to be recognised.

Reilly thought there something familiar about the man's gait, but could not place it. But, he felt, if he might know this person, perhaps he was in league with Lloyd George and Reilly wanted to discover the meaning of this summit.

He waited a sufficient time and then went to the front door. Reilly knocked and quietly subdued the butler when he opened it. He then followed the voices. With the door closed, he couldn't make out who was in that room nor what was being said. But he removed his pistol from his overcoat and held it at the ready.

After a moment, the door opened very slowly as Lloyd George backed out of the room, still calling for the butler. As Lloyd George emerged fully, but with the door not completely ajar, Reilly put his pistol to the back of Lloyd George's head and would have pulled the trigger had he not heard a familiar voice shouting, "My God, Reilly, no! No!"

Reilly looked into the room to see that it was, indeed, Holmes. He kept the pistol close to Lloyd George's head, cocking the trigger and pushing Lloyd George back into the room. However, the pistol in Lloyd George's hand was still aimed at Holmes.

Even through Holmes' entreaties, Reilly would not lower his pistol. Nor would Lloyd George lower his.

Then, suddenly, Reilly felt the cold barrel of a pistol stuck into the back of his own head. The other pistol was in the hand of Bugsy Siegel.

Siegel looked at Holmes and said, "Hey, Johhny! I been followin' ya since this mornin'. When all these other mugs showed up I figured I better get inside and protect my investment, right?"

In retrospect, the vision of Siegel holding a gun on Reilly holding a gun on Lloyd George holding a gun on Holmes is quite amusing. And it would become even more so because Siegel had just called Holmes 'Johnny'. You can imagine the confusion as pistols continued to be pointed:

Reilly: 'Johnny?'

Lloyd George: 'Who?'

Siegel: 'Johnny.'

Reilly: "He's Holmes!'

Siegel: "Who?'

Lloyd George: "Holmes.'

Reilly: "Holmes."

Holmes, resignedly: "Holmes."

Siegel: 'Holmes? I thought you were Clay. Who the hell is Holmes and then who the hell are these guys? What the…?'

To be sure, they could have gone around like that for hours, but there were three pistols being wielded, one of which was aimed at Holmes. He finally ended this stalemate by imploring everyone to put their pistols down and to sit down so he could explain.   They did, and he did. But with the three still holding their pistols at ready; though not at their chosen target.

Holmes explained that against his strongest impulses and those of Reilly, Lloyd George must be set free for Watson's sake. Holmes, must, of course, keep silent because he cannot do otherwise. To have Holmes suddenly reappear in the midst of London, too much would have to be explained and there was no telling how much might be exposed.

Reilly was all for killing Lloyd George anyway and spiriting the entire Watson family to safety afterwards. And Siegel was for killing him on general principle though he hadn't the faintest idea of what was going on.

However, Holmes' cooler head prevailed. All warily arose and put their pistols away.

Lloyd George left immediately and went straight to his home because he had to be sure that his plan for Watson was still in place.

With Lloyd George gone, and the butler still unconscious, but beginning to regain his senses, Holmes suggested that they all take a brief walk to a quiet pub where they could have a beverage and Ben and Reilly could become better acquainted. Especially later, when Siegel found out that Reilly was really Jewish.

Holmes' auto followed behind.

Holmes And Reilly And Bugsy

They repaired to *The Bulldog's Rump*, Holmes explaining, when they were comfortably seated, that this had once figured prominently in one of his cases when he was a consulting detective. However, I had not written about this particular mystery, which is why *The Bulldog's Rump* has not achieved, until now, any prominence.

"Yeah, but you're workin' with us now, Johnny," Siegel said after his first sip of ale which he almost spit all over the table.

"Horse piss! What the hell's with this horse piss?"

"Ben, it's ale. In England we drink it at room temperature."

"Hey buddy," Siegel called to the bartender, "you got any cold American beer?"

"Sure 'nuff, mate. Comin' up."

"How the hell dya drink that stuff? You drive on the wrong side of the road and ya drink horse piss. You limeys are nuts."

"After what happened tonight, Ben, I won't argue the point," Reilly said.

The barkeep brought Siegel a cold beer which he immediately sipped with obvious relief.

"Yeah, now let me get this straight," Siegel asked Reilly, "just how the hell did a Jew get a mick name?"

"That, my new-found friend is a story in itself," Reilly answered. "Would you care to hear about my forebears?"

"You got four bears? What the hell you doin' with four bears?"

"No, Ben, my mother and father."

"They got four bears?"

"Precisely," Reilly finally said, not wishing this to continue.

"Yeah, well how about tellin' me how you and Johnny hooked up while I drink my beer."

"Whatever you'd like, Ben. Holmes, or rather, Johnny, here, and I met when we went to save the Tsar and his family from being executed by the Bolsheviks. And we succeeded, too. And Johnny, here, along with the Royal Navy, brought them to a beautiful island in the Caribbean and they all lived happily ever after."

"You crappin' me, right?"

"Ben, it's the absolute truth, so help me, Adonai," Reilly said.

Siegel just looked at him, then Holmes, who shook his head that this was, in fact true.

"You're both nuts. You expect me to believe crap like that? Like I believe in Santa Claus and the tooth fairy and the Easter bunny and I got a nice bridge in Brooklyn I can sell you two."

Siegel and Reilly laughed, but Holmes just watched. He knew that Reilly would not have returned to London without a very compelling reason, and he was anxious to find out what it was. But he wanted Siegel and Reilly to become better acquainted. He had an idea that had come to him while the three sat there in *The Bulldog's Rump*, and he wanted to see how these men got on.

Two hours passed, personal histories were exchanged, but who could tell what was truth or tall tale while cold beer and warm ale continued to arrive with merry regularity.

"Now, this is the god's honest truth," Siegel said as he unfolded, very proudly, how he had dispatched two men with one bullet. It demonstrated perfectly how he acquired his nickname and just how dangerous an adversary he could be.

"When Meyer and me had our gang, before Meyer decided it was best to hook up with Charlie and his gang, we had some dagos who was cuttin' in on our gamblin' activities. This was way before Numbers Malone and his boys tried the same thing.

"Now, Meyer may be short, but he's as tough as they come. There ain't nothin' that scares Meyer. Not even Charlie. So Meyer figures that we wait for these guys at one of the bookie joints what takes the bets and gives us our cuts.

"So in comes Rico Abato and Marco Pavese and they tell the bookie t' fork over the dough. The bookie is dumpin' bricks because he's between two tough dagos with guns and two tough Jews with guns.

"Meyer comes walkin' in from the back with a bottle of beer, all calm like and asks the dagos what they want. Well right away, they tell Meyer t' get the hell out or they'll kill him; and they call him a mockey midget.

"Meyer slams the bottle against the face of Rico, who falls back into Marco and they both fall on the floor and Rico is screaming and Marco is tryin' t' get out from under Rico.

"Then I come out from the back, push Rico back so his head is right in front of Marco's and I put one bullet through both their heads at the same time. Like Buffalo Bill. Pretty nice, huh?"

Reilly and Holmes marveled at Siegel's unbridled pride in murder; but for quite different reasons. While Holmes had spent a good portion of his life helping the police capture such homicidal maniacs, and was ill at ease with the sheer brutality of Siegel's act, Reilly, with a professional view, admired it. And he, more than Holmes, understood completely.

Perhaps it was because of his darker persona that so closely mirrored Sigel's, but Reilly felt compelled to tell his own story.

"Gentlemen, "Reilly said, savoring the moment, "what I'm about to disclose, no one has ever heard of before. No one."

"Holy crap, this must really be somethin'," Siegel said, sipping his beer excitedly. Holmes already knew Reilly's capabilities in divergent directions, but was still taken aback at what he was about to hear.

"Who I was working for at the time doesn't matter. What matters is that the person I was assigned to dispatch was a high clergyman of a religion I need not name.

"It seems that this paradigm of virtue was selling, yes, I said 'selling', young boys and girls to the Ottomans to do with as they pleased. Even had the authorities been alerted, with such an exalted personage, it seemed nothing would've been done.

"But there was no error. I was shown proof and I believed what I saw. So one night, as our paradigm slept, I gained access to his room, my feet and shoes in Wellingtons, my hands in rubber gloves, I put one extra thin blanket over him and dispatched him with one dagger thrust deep into his heart. I then sliced open his chest at that point.

"I next severed his male appendage and put it where his heart was and left as I had come; first putting the Wellingtons and the gloves into a sack, then tossing them into a safe disposal point far from where I had been."

Silence. Even from Siegel who just stared. Holmes' head was down.

"Damn, even I ain't never done nothin' like that," Siegel said, with a mixture of awe and revulsion.

"That was then, Ben. We all do things when we're young we may regret when we're older. Isn't that right, Holmes?"

Holmes lifted his head, shaking it slightly. "Most assuredly."

It was the perfect time for Siegel to call it a night.

"After what you just said, and nobody lettin' me bump off that Lloyd George guy, I've come to the conclusion that you guys are all crazy here. Nobody kills nobody even when

194

they need to get dead. Meyer and Lucky are never gonna believe all this crap!

"I'm gonna go back to New York and give the guys one hell of a laugh about what's goin' on over here. Especially when they find out that Clay is really Holmes and I got a Jewish pal named Reilly. They'll think I'm nuts; but then, everyone does anyway.

"But don't worry, Johnny, I'll tell 'em all the books are square and the booze is comin' to nobody but Charlie and Meyer and me and we'll all make a toast t' you over here. Or maybe an English muffin instead o' toast. Pretty good, huh? Toast, English muffin, get it?"

He then extended his hand to Reilly.

"From now on, your name is Moo."

"I don't get it," Reilly said, completely baffled as Siegel laughed.

"It's what ya get when ya cross a mick with a Jew. Ya get a Moo. You're Moo."

Reilly laughed, too, and said, "Ben, if it makes you happy, I'm Moo," and they shook hands.

With that, Siegel left the pub, hailed a cab, went back to the Cumberland, and had a good night's sleep before preparing for his departure to New York. But he still shook his head at the seeming insanity of no one killing anyone else.

Holmes And Reilly

Holmes sat with Reilly, still unsettled at his story. Reilly saw this and said, "Holmes, did you actually believe that tale I just told?"

"Yes."

"Well, as Ben said, I've got a bridge in Brooklyn I'd like to sell you." And he laughed.

Holmes was now left to wondering which was true; and to him, that was even more unsettling. But he and Reilly still had much to discuss and that could continue the next day.

They walked to the curb, Holmes signaled and his auto pulled up, driven by Andrew. As Reilly and Holmes got into the rear and Holmes closed the glass partition, Andrews's eyes, looking in his rearview mirror, suddenly opened wide.

"Well, Holmes, I hadn't expected to see you again."

"Nor I, you. At least, so soon."

"It may be the ale talking, but just think, Holmes, of all I've been through since I left you in Russia." He began counting them off in a most cavalierly manner.

"I spent some leisurely time trying to foment a counter-revolution, becoming an ally of Trotsky, an enemy of a pig you never heard of, Stalin, being chased out of Russia and across Finland, back to London, then to Eleuthera, then back to this very spot."

"I am sure there are details you have omitted since we spoke in New York."

"Yes. Very unhappy details." He told of the almost simultaneous deaths of Alexei and the Tsarina, which was the reason for his return for revenge against Lloyd George.

However he thought it best to reveal nothing about the Grand Duchesses' whereabouts and current identities.

He then turned his body as much as possible to face Holmes. "Holmes, I know we spoke of this in New York, but what about Watson?"

"Reilly, let me tell you what Lloyd George and I were discussing when you and he met, shall we say." He then disclosed all.

"If I made myself manifest by even the most meager method to Watson, what further danger might befall Watson?" Holmes asked.

"With Lloyd George as Prime Minister, with all the power he had, and the "Black Faction" and the "invisible others" who so plagued our endeavors in Russia and thereafter, it is even too much for me to try to unravel. Especially on the heels of what he just disclosed. No, it is best that all is left as Watson believes."

Reilly sat pensively. "Yes, you're right, I suppose. But Holmes, you're a national hero. Sunk by the Huns. Did you swim back to London?"

"There was no ship sunk. Captain Yardley saved my life. But I'll retain that for another telling."

Holmes then related the events of his rescue by the Curtis family.

"Curtis? Did you say Curtis?"

Holmes was startled at the reaction. "Yes, the three men who rescued me."

"By any chance, would two of those men be named Louis and Martin?"

"Now how could you possibly know that?"

Reilly was laughing. "As I believe you've said from time to time, 'elementary'." And he laughed more loudly.

Holmes was becoming annoyed at Reilly laughing at his expense. "All right, all right, how did you know?"

"Holmes, remember that little town you were brought to when you were rescued?"

"Port Royal."

"Then you know that Port Royal is the closest town to Parris Island, the east coast training ground for the United States Marine Corps. Many of the senior Marine Corps. officers live there. Some still on active duty, some retired."

"Yes, but how did you know about Lou and Martin Curtis?"

"Lou and Martin were captains in the Corps. and were serving in G-2, their military intelligence.

"Before the States got into the war, President Wilson and their top brass wanted to see how we might integrate our forces if they got into the war; so Lou and Martin were sent over with others to London surreptitiously.

"I met them, oddly enough, at a cocktail party being hosted by Kitchener as War Minister. It wasn't too long after the party that his cruiser hit a German mine and he drowned when the ship sank."

"Did you have dealings with them?"

"All I can say is 'yes', I had dealings with them. But I can't disclose them. What I can disclose is that you couldn't want for two more steadfast friends or implacable foes. They're best of the Yankee breed."

"But what of their father, Hank?"

"I don't know anything about him. But I wouldn't be surprised that he had some special assignment during the war, too."

They had arrived at Holmes lair and Reilly had the usual astonishment at the building and the decay surrounding.

"Welcome to my domain," Holmes said, making a sweeping gesture with his arms indicating the area around. "Come with me." Holmes pointed up, to where his office was.

Reilly now felt that he had been correct in New York. This was not the Sherlock Holmes who had proved so brilliant in Russia. This was another man entirely. But he felt that he had no choice. He needed to learn all and so he followed Holmes up those stairs.

Once in Holmes' office and long on into the night, Holmes told Reilly of his involvement with Siegel, Luciano, and Lansky and his international criminal network. But Reilly couldn't understand why he was being told these things.

And hours before, neither Holmes nor Reilly had noticed Andrew glancing back at them as he had driven them to Whitechapel.

The Grand Duchess of New York

Olga, now Katherine Kasey, had purchased a cooperative on the wealthy and thriving upper west side of Manhattan, right on Central Park West, at number 55, a classic Art Deco residential tower. Not too distant from the flat once owned by Capone.

Olga was in love with New York as a whole, but with Manhattan, in particular. No city, to her mind, could possibly be more vibrant and alive than this. She was throwing off every inhibition and moral manacle, choosing a more merry and exuberant existence than she could have dreamed of in her former cloistered world.

Manhattan was the epicenter of The Roaring Twenties; and please forgive the play on words, but Olga was in her twenties and roaring like a young lioness.

Nightlife was utmost. And nightlife during Prohibition meant speakeasies. And speakeasies, at least the best ones, meant the underworld. And that meant that any beautiful and apparently rich young woman, such as Olga, would attract certain eyes. Certain big blue eyes. Big blue eyes that belonged to Bugsy Siegel.

Reilly Says "Hello" And "Goodbye"

It was the night after the Holmes-Lloyd George-Reilly-Siegel incident, that Reilly knocked on my door for the third time.

It had been two years or so since last I saw him and he had much to tell; and, I surmised, much not to tell. But what he chose to tell was, he believed, that which would set my mind at rest.

He told me that Holmes had indeed perished; not by the perfidious hand of his own government, but as a true hero of England. His ship, had, in fact, been sunk by the Germans. Reilly felt that this would give me surcease, which it did, and I thanked him for the information; at that time not knowing the true volume of this most magnanimous deception.

After that, he told me of the tragic events on Eleuthera, of the health and beauty of little Sidney, but not of the whereabouts of the Grand Duchesses. I was to learn of their subsequent histories only much later; but which I have already put forth for more facile chronology.

Finally, it was time for Reilly to depart once more. And this time, we both thought we would never see each other again.

How tragically wrong we were.

Marie Meets The Admiral

Marie and William were to be married. Though she, as a Romanov Grand Duchess, was brought up in the strictest of Russian Orthodoxy, she consented, for love of William, to become Anglican.

That obstacle overcome, William, as with a little boy pleading with his mother for more time to play before dinner, begged Marie to have a wedding in the Royal Navy manner. This would be performed by a Royal Navy chaplain; with William's closest fellow officers in attendance to provide the swords-crossed arch under which they would pass for good luck. Marie consented, but only if she was to be a June bride. And so the date was set: Saturday, June 24, 1923.

However, there was one small formality that had not, as yet, been attended. Admiral Yardley had not met Marie; or, rather, Mary. As far as he knew, William was marrying a quite wealthy young woman named Mary Hampton, and that her sister, Anna, was to be her Maid of Honour. Mary's parents had long ago passed on.

William introduced Marie to his father over dinner at one of London's most fashionable restaurants at the time, Frascati's, on Oxford Street. Admiral Yardley, of course, approved and was especially taken with Marie's bearing, composure and intelligence.

"So, Mary, William tells me you met in Grosvenor Square." This was true, of course, but not chronologically.

"Why, yes. William was so dashing in his naval uniform that when he touched the bill of his cap in gentlemanly salute, how could I not respond with a smile and a nod of my head?" William looked at her with eyebrows raised and an askew smile in appreciation of her happy fib.

"And then one thing led to another." They all laughed.

"I certainly see," Admiral Yardley said.

"And I'm very happy for that," William said, as he bent towards Marie and kissed her cheek.

"Admiral," said Marie, "there's a question I would like to put to you, one that even William doesn't know of."

William and his father exchanged glances indicating curiosity and the Admiral replied, "Of, course, Mary, anything you would like."

"As you know, my parents have passed on," she was trying to present this in a formal manner as if she were still acting as a Grand Duchess, "it would mean the world to me if you would take the place of my father, and give me away. Would that be possible?"

The smiles on the faces of the Admiral and William instantly changed to those of serious surprise. Tears fell from the Admiral's eyes as he took Marie's hand and said, "Mary, I can't possibly take the place of your beloved father, but I'll be honoured to not only give you away, but to take you into our family at the same time."

Marie was now crying and even William, seeing Marie and his father so tearfully joyous, felt his cheeks growing moist. So he stopped this moment of sentimentality with a jocular, "Now isn't that nice? The Lord giveth and taketh away!" They all began laughing as Marie and the Admiral dried their tears.

It was a truly happy evening and for once, it appeared that nothing could mar the occasion.

Outside Frascati's, waiting in his auto, was a man who had learned of the presence in London of Marie and Anastasia. But he had done so in the following Holmesian manner; direct and circuitous in unison.

Based upon what Reilly had divulged, he surmised that two of the Grand Duchesses had come to London. By carefully examining the passenger lists of all the ocean liners which had docked in England at not-too distant dates preceding Reilly's arrival, then examining the lists of which ships disembarked from the Bahamas in like interval to New York, then examining those lists for synonymous names of women on both, it was a small matter to discover their new names and then their current addresses.

The man in the auto was, of course, Holmes. And if Reilly had not said anything to him about the Grand Duchesses' presence in London, he understood why. He further understood that Marie and Anastasia might need some looking after; which he had certain men assigned to do. They knew nothing other than to keep a watchful on two special friends of Mr. Stash.

But this night, the first night that he had come to see Marie personally, he was astonished to see William Yardley with her. Then he remembered what happened on Eleuthera and he was pleased.

He now had an even more felicitous reason to repay young Yardley. And
in a way that would have very special meaning for both Yardley and Marie.

My Growing Fame

While all the above was unfolding not too distant from my front door, Elizabeth, John and I were going about with our own quiet lives. Nothing out of the ordinary had interrupted our routine: me with patients seeking succor from maladies true and false; Elizabeth with duties as mother and keeper of the Watson residence; and John studying diligently, not unlike his father in that respect.

He was hoping to become a physician, too, and nothing could have given his mother and me greater joy. It was assumed that he, as had I, would seek his medical training at the University of London when of proper enrollment age.

Though my income as a physician alone would have given us all a quite comfortable life, I had unwittingly carved out another profession for myself as the chronicler of all things Sherlock Holmes.

Holmes had already, through my accounts of his adventures, become an important public figure in England. But with his selfless death in service of King and country, he had become a national hero.

He had become something of a fad. There were other Holmes books by unauthorized authors, of course, but there were Holmes postcards, tea cups, beer mugs, umbrellas, a line of clothing imitating his inimitable fashion statements, or lack thereof, in my opinion; even pet accoutrements.

Anything that could bear a visage of Holmes or large enough to bear his name, was sure to carry one, the other, or both. There were even Sherlock Holmes motion pictures, for heaven's sake; but from which I also received a small royalty.

It was the stipends I received from my endeavors regarding Holmes that formed the basis of our financial security.

I was feted and celebrated as the man closest to Holmes, almost discounting entirely the existence of his true brother, Mycroft. But Mycroft didn't seem to mind, at all. In fact, over a long and pleasant dinner heavy with spirits and good will, he said, "Not for me this colossal hoopla, over my brother, Watson. No, better you than me."

Besides my accounts of the mysteries Holmes had solved, I was retained to give in-depth lectures about Holmes, as if I were an Etonian professor discoursing on various and sundry members of the Ancient Greek pantheon of mythological beings. Then, I was signed to a contract by one of the nation's most prominent speaker agencies, the Herbert A. Miles Agency.

At first, my lectures were limited to London. Then throughout the United Kingdom. Soon enough, I was traveling through a still re-building Europe. But as my ventures into the world became longer, Elizabeth and I decided that with John away at school, it would be happiest for us both if she would travel with me should my speaking schedule demand my absence from home for any great length of time. This we did, though we never did reach the Orient or India; which I longed to   revisit.

Shortly, I was asked by Herbert if I would consider a lengthy lecture series in Canada and the United States. Dare I say that Elizabeth had the bags packed before I could agree?

The lecture itinerary would be thus: Montreal, Toronto, Winnipeg, Vancouver, San Francisco, Los Angeles, Chicago,

Washington D.C. Boston, New York, then back home. We would be gone two whole months and we would be traveling first class via ocean liner, railway and motorcar all the way; as always part of my fee negotiated by Herbert.

But the pace would be grueling and had Elizabeth not been by my side for counsel and care, I'm not sure how well I would have held up.

We set sail on the fabulous RMS *Olympic* on Saturday, the twenty-fourth of June, 1923. And had we an atom of knowledge of the infamous event we would witness in New York, we never would have gone.

A Royal Wedding

The wedding of Marie and William went as happily as anyone would want. The twenty-fourth of June was sunnier than usual, but a bit cooler, too; William's shipmates provided the drawn-swords arch, Anastasia served as Maid of Honour, rice was thrown, cheers were loud, lusty and long and anyone could see that the couple loved each other deeply. The Admiral could take solace knowing that this would be a truly happy union.

The only unmelodic note came from Anastasia. Of late, Marie had noticed that her sister seemed to be even more subdued than usual; more introspective and dour. She couldn't focus on her duties as Maid of Honour and wasn't present for the wedding rehearsal. But she apologised when she reappeared and begged forgiveness because of a minor illness.

Marie was concerned, of course, but with wedding arrangement to be attended, and honeymoon plans to be made, she believed Anastasia was still grieving for Alexei, understood and hoped that Anastasia would soon become her former happy self.

But during the wedding, when the chaplain asked if anyone there objected to the union, Anastasia had muttered quietly but audibly enough for those close to hear, "Yurovsky"; the name of the commandant of the Ipatiev House in Ekaterinburg, where the Romanovs had been held for execution, until rescued by Holmes, Reilly and me.

Marie, whose hand was holding William's, tightened so firmly that he winced in pain. Then Anastasia coughed, which gave verity that the utterance previous was only a cough.

The ceremony now completed with no further incident, the couple hurried into a celebratory hansom cab and were swiftly trotted off to Marie's home, which was now William's, as well. From there, all packed and pleased and plucky, they left for their honeymoon; which would be only one week because William, still on duty, could not take much leave. But it did not matter, so completely happy were the two.

As they were driven out of sight of their home by a pre-engaged cab, and the domestics had ceased their congratulatory waving of handkerchiefs and returned inside, a man quietly opened the front door so the domestics would not hear, and went no further in than two paces. There, he left a small, exquisitely wrapped box on the table which would normally receive gloves and such.

He then withdrew as quietly as he had come.

Anastasia Vanishes

On Eleuthera, the family was very happy.

The Tsar found great solace in little Sidney, and with Reilly having returned the May previous, there was a further feeling of safety.

Adding to the great joy of everyone, on February 7, 1923, a sister was provided for little Sidney, named Alix; a combination of both departed loved ones' names: Alexandra and Alexei. Olga, Marie and Anastasia were notified in code.

While Reilly had wanted, at first, to keep the sisters from communicating at all, that had been proved impractical. So with the special communication shack at the compound attended sporadically by still-serving sergeants, Olga and Marie had been able to keep in touch with the family, but not directly with each other; all in code only the family would understand.

It was in that context that they received a disturbing wire from Marie in July: Anastasia had vanished.

Red Or White?

In Paris, there was quite a stir amidst the intellectual and arts community. It seemed that a beautiful young woman had surfaced. Of course, beautiful young women were always surfacing in Paris. But this one was different. This one claimed to be the Grand Duchess Anastasia Nicolayevna Romanova, the youngest daughter of the last Tsar.

Parisians, as had the world, presumed her to have been killed, along with her entire family, by the Bolsheviks at the Ipatiev House in Ekaterinburg

Anastasia had Paris jumping through preposterous hoops. The city was divided between pro and anti-Anastasia factions. Street fights were fought. Death oaths were taken. Émigré whites and rabid reds were ready to tear Paris to tatters. Anastasia was having the best time of her life. But in reality, the poor thing had finally and entirely unraveled.

However, she had, at least, enough common sense to retain funds with which to live; albeit modestly. She rented a small studio at 16 Place-du-Tertre, tucked away to the west of Sacre Coeur, in Montmartre. The area was filled with artists and intellectuals who could argue any side of an argument and would do so just for the intellectual and emotional exercise.

Anastasia provided many such exercises.

The city was filled with Russian émigrés, refugees of the revolution. There were true nobles and others claiming to have been so. It seemed they all had stories to prove they were high-born aristocrats, but only a few had the funds to live as such. Particularly in Arrondissement de Passy; one of the most expensive and beautiful areas of Paris in which to dwell.

The ones who claimed that their fortunes had been confiscated by the Bolsheviks, or never had any fortunes to begin with, lived in the more impoverished areas of Paris to the northeast, like Sevran.

Those of the émigrés who had an artistic bent, flowed to the right bank and Montmartre, right where Anastasia was living.

It seemed as if all the whites were trying to claim her as their own. They would arrive at her tiny studio either in chauffeur-driven Bugatti Royales, by tram, or foot and invariably it would be the same: "Anastasia! You remember me, don't you?" Then some event would be named that, of course, should have rung the bell in Anastasia's mind.

But no bells rang. In fact, she rarely spoke. She seemed to prefer to listen to the people prattle on, accepting whatever gift they offered, with a vacuous smile; be it valuable or otherwise.

Then there were the bon vivants and the boulevardiers who came calling on the supposedly beautiful twenty-four-year-old Romanov Grand Duchess. Vultures circling, nothing more. Although, to this day, no romance has ever been attached to Anastasia.

And though all manner of cognoscenti tried, no one could quite get precise information on just how she had escaped the firing squad nor if any of her family had survived, as well.

The reds did nothing, really, other than argue with the whites that the Romanovs were dead and buried, that this girl was obviously an escapee from some insane asylum and that bolshevism or communism, or whichever "ism" they chose, would soon conquer the world.

Yes, Anastasia was a mystery; and in a city like Paris, or any city, for that matter, who does not enjoy a good mystery.

Until her return from their honeymoon, Marie had tried to banish any thought of Anastasia and what she had said at the wedding. To a degree, because of her happiness with William, she had succeeded.

But she also vowed that once back from Brighton, where they were spending their honeymoon, she would confront Anastasia and discover what truly troubled her and to see if she could help.

Upon their arrival home and receipt of more smiles and congratulations from the domestics and as their luggage were being taken to be unpacked, Marie noticed that little box on the entry table.

"William, there's a beautiful little box here for you; look. It has a card with your name on it."

William took the box. It was wrapped in a most expensive paper, with intricately painted designs adorning. It was tied with fine silk ribbon. He looked at his name and asked Marie if the writing looked familiar. She said "no".

"Well, then. It's not big enough for a bomb, so I guess I'll just have to open it." But before he pulled the silk ribbon, he looked at Marie, "Are you sure this isn't from you?"

"No, really, William. I just saw it here this second." She asked a domestic walking down the hallway if she or anyone knew who the box was from.

"No, ma'am. Funny, after you and the Captain had just left for your honeymoon, we saw the box there, but none of us knew how it got there. So we just left it there since it has the Captain's name on it. We figured it was a wedding present. Perhaps a surprise from you for him when you returned."

"May I open it now," William asked, anxiously.

"Yes, yes, go ahead," Marie said, playfully pushing him.

Upon doing so, he untied the ribbon, carefully unfolded the paper, which revealed a small, solid mahogany box with gold leaf around the edges. Then he opened the box and when he removed the delicate contents, Marie fainted.

Olga And Bugsy

In New York, Olga had fallen in love with Bemjamin Siegel, and, it seemed, he with her.

"Ya can't find a nice Jewish girl?" Lansky asked, hitting Siegel in the head when Siegel told about his feelings.

"Hey, Meyer. I can't have kosher all the time, ya know," Siegel replied.

"How about a nice Italian girl? What's wrong with Italian girls?" Luciano needled.

"They cook so good I'll blow up like a balloon and look like Masseria. No thank you, Charlie."

He knew he was in love with his "shiksa British broad". She even calmed him down. But only slightly.

There was no need of Olga to ask questions of Benjamin. She already knew about who he was, what he did, and that added to the thrill. As for Siegel, since he didn't like questions asked about him or his friends, he didn't ask anything of Katherine.

She had already told him that her parents were deceased and that she had no siblings. And as far as Siegel could determine, even with some of his lawyers trying to glean information on her, nothing untoward surfaced. They reported that she was wealthy, British, and, "Ben, have a good time."

It looked like Katherine Kasey would soon become Katherine Siegel.

In that regard, Tatiana received a wire from Olga, which she read to Reilly after decoding.

"Tatiana. I have finally met and fallen in love with someone. I assure you, though, I have told him nothing of us.

215

"This is a man of mystery. A powerful man. A feared man. A man who will protect me and care for me and love me."

Reilly, smiling at the happy news, and holding both Sidney and Alix, asked innocently, "And who is this American paragon?"

Tatiana said, "She says his name is Siegel. Benjamin Siegel."

Reilly put the children down, told Tatiana that he would explain presently, ran to find Funny Oscar and then went to make arrangements, as soon as possible, to go to New York.

Not wanting to worry Tatiana, nor the Tsar, he told them that his reason for leaving so precipitously was that he knew this Benjamin Siegel and that while a fine, upstanding man, there had been some unfortunate history with his family and he felt it best to speak with Olga as soon as possible to personally try to dissuade her from this relationship.

The Tsar seemed to accept the explanation without question, but Tatiana knew her husband too well.

"Sidney, there's more to this than you're telling us, isn't there?"

"Tatiana, please believe me, I think only I can prevent a marriage and it needs to be prevented."

"Is it that bad?" Tatiana asked.

Still trying to mitigate her fear, he said, "Well, not that bad, but enough to cause us all a headache we most certainly don't need."

Tatiana finally accepted that and the next day, once more stood on the dock waving off her husband. This time with Alix accompanying little Sidney in bawling their unhappiness.

The Meaning Of The Gift

When Marie regained her senses through smelling salts immediately administered by William, he asked, "Mary, what happened? Are you all right?"

He had carried her into the drawing room and sat beside her on a comfortable divan. Now that she was revived, he gestured for the concerned domestics to leave them alone and close the door; which they did.

"William, the gift to you…"

"What of it? Did this little gold wrist chain cause you to faint?"

"Yes, William. Don't you know what that is?"

"I haven't the faintest clue in the world."

She spoke haltingly, frightened.

"William, just before Holmes left us on Eleuthera and joined you on the ship, my father took that off his wrist and gave it to Holmes in thanks. It had been given to my father by his mother and it was the last thing of any personal value he had to give."

William looked confused.

"It means, William, that Holmes is alive and he's given you that gift in the same spirit as my father had."

William then understood. But he couldn't say anything to her about Holmes. So he asked Marie, still sobbing softly, to put the delicate gold chain on his right wrist.

She did this gently, happily, and felt that her father was now with her, as well.

Revenge

Holmes' psyche had been slowly gnawed at in his incarnation as Clay. It had always razor-thin and fragile, even in the best of times, but now it had reached a level of danger.

Since he could not, as yet, exact revenge on Lloyd George and had to let him live, he was feeling claustrophobic. Even his criminal kingdom stretching from the United Kingdom to the United States and beyond, was now too small of a palette on which his mind could paint.

If Lloyd George must live, Holmes needed one magnificent, grandiose offence against him that would, simultaneously, give Holmes the identities of the men tasked to do me harm and cause Lloyd George such horrific embarrassment and shame from which he might never recover.

But that was not all. Holmes wanted this crime committed so that no one would even know that a crime had been committed. Only that could placate his mind and soul and psyche; and his revenge would be sadistically satisfied

His statement to Lloyd George, "God, as devil incarnate, has devised more than one way to blot out the sun," gave him the answer; and he devised his plan.

He would blot out the sun by becoming the sun. Using his disguise skills nonpareil, he would become Lloyd George.

Holmes had long studied his routines, his personal matters, he knew of his club, his solicitor, his bank, his accountant; in short, everything he would need to exact a revenge different than originally sought. But one, perhaps, much more mollifying.

On the night of August 29, 1923, Lloyd George stepped to the curb outside his home and signaled for his auto, got in, then realized something was wrong. His driver was not his driver. It was a stranger; in reality, one of Holmes' men. Others jumped in and blindfolded him. He was then driven to an abandoned house not far from Holmes' headquarters in Whitechapel. They then dragged him out, brought him into a room and left.

Inside this hovel, in a room with two wooden chairs and one table with a glass of water on it, Holmes sat on one of the chairs; but with a grotesque Renaissance mask covering his features as Mr. Stash, since Lloyd George had already seen him.

At first, Lloyd George was screaming and indignant. He demanded of this bizarre apparition before him if he knew who he was. Holmes said nothing.

Then he demanded to know what was wanted of him. Holmes said nothing.

Finally, after pacing and puffing and pulling at the locked door, and screaming and demanding, his energy waned and he sat in the other chair and sipped the water.

Finally, Holmes spoke; but with a non-descript accent.

"I know who you are, Prime Minister. But I've been retained by an anonymous gentleman to take care of this needlessly messy business."

"Who is this so-called gentleman?" Lloyd George demanded.

Mr. Stash flashed anger.

"It is not for you to be asking a question of me. It is for you to answer a question from me. And it is a simple one.

"I have been asked to give you a choice. You may choose a swift and painless death if you give me the information I want, or so thoroughly a disagreeable one that I shiver to think of it, should you not."

"Who are you?" demanded Lloyd George, again.

Mr. Stash became enraged.

"I said you do not ask any questions. You anger me and it causes me grief."

By now, Lloyd George did not know what to make of this mad man but decided it might be best to give him the information he wanted as long as it was not most secret.

"All right. What information do you want?"

Mr. Stash immediately became more tranquil and even the tone of his voice became soothing.

"Just this: who is the person, or persons, you have told to kill Dr. John H. Watson should any harm befall you?"

"Holmes! I knew it! That blackguard!"

Mr. Stash now kicked the chair violently; but not Lloyd George.

"Are you deaf? Do you not understand? I shall not ask you again. Who is the person, or persons, you have given that special command to?"

With great reluctance, Lloyd George gave Holmes the code names of two men in a special branch; one which caused Holmes to cry out, "Fool! Damned fool that I am."

His men ran in in alarm thinking Mr. Stash had gone mad but Holmes made gestures to bring these events to a swift conclusion. Holmes took possession of Lloyd George's identification papers and he and his men left the room. Lloyd George remained locked in that room overnight. But unharmed.

The first code name he gave Holmes was Andrew.

The other was Yrjö.

Holmes then sent two of his men to bring Andrew to him. In short order, they had done so. Andrew was calm, having no idea what Holmes wanted.

"So, Andrew," said Holmes, mask removed and again Mr. Stash, "you've been keeping secrets from me."

"I don' know wha' ya mean, Mr. Stash," Andrew said in his guttural rasp.

"I see, well perhaps this might refresh your retrograde memory." Holmes showed him an identification paper of Lloyd George's. Andrew knew he was trapped but sought to bargain his way out of death.

"All right, Mr. Stash, you've found me out." He was speaking perfectly now.

"But what have I found out exactly, Andrew."

"Mr. Stash, I've work for a special branch of intelligence since Lloyd George was Prime Minister. I was assigned special tasks by him then which would carry over even after he left office. That's the way special orders work in special branches."

"Yes, but what brings you to my employ?" Holmes asked wanting more answers more quickly.

"Well, that's easy enough. The Yanks asked us to help stop the flow of alcohol to them because of their Prohibition. I was assigned to help do that. We knew that Clay was behind the shipments, but since nobody sees him anymore, it devolved upon you as the focal point of my investigation."

"And what have you learned, Andrew?"

"Everything you're doing, Mr.Stash. I can't hide that fact. But the funny thing is, no matter what I reported, nobody ever gave the order to bring down the hammer on you. Pretty curious."

"Not so, when one may have special friends in the special branch."

Andrew's eyes grew wide in sudden understanding. He fumbled as other words came out.

"Uh, uh, Mr. Stash, one other thing. That night that I drove you away from that house with that other man. I think I know who he is. I worked with him once, but I thought he was dead. I could tell you all about him."

Holmes stopped this immediately by asking one all-important question.

"Tell me, Andrew, those special orders you had, one about eliminating a certain Dr. Watson, was there anyone else under such orders?"

"Now, how the hell did you know about that?" Andrew asked.

"Special friends…"

"Yes, I see. No, I don't know of anyone else under that order. I really don't." "Andrew, you will be permitted to live, but that is all."

He gave a signal to the men who had brought him in and as they took hold of him,

Holmes said "You know where to bring him. Do it, but don't harm him. Just bind him and leave him there." This they did.

As they left him alone, Holmes wondered if he truly was now more Clay than Holmes; and shuddered. But he still had much to do that night. The best part of his plan was about to unfold.

First, he shaved all his facial hair and disguised himself as Lloyd George. He knew that if Lloyd George did not return home or spend the night at his club, the National Liberal Club, his domestics would become alarmed and suspicious. Therefore, he checked into the club and had word sent to his home that he would be spending the night there and would return the next day.

As Mr. Stash, Holmes knew many members of the club from surreptitious and unsavory business arrangements; but he was now Lloyd George.

Having whiskeys with these fellow club members individually, he let it be known very quietly to those he thought would be most amenable, that he might be able to arrange knighthoods, and, in some instances, even a peerage or two, for a proper consideration.

Some of these gullibles immediately gave cheques to Holmes while others pledged funds to be deposited in his accounts by the morrow. But he had also made overtures to men he knew to be above reproach and who would, when the time was right, make these offers publicly known.

In the morning, once Lloyd George's bank was open, Holmes left the club, went to the bank and had the bank manager deposit the collected cheques in Lloyd George's account; taking special care to engage him in a lively conversation which the manager would must certainly remember and recount to investigative authorities.

Holmes also knew that the other men who had promised monies to Lloyd George would also be round to deposit those funds with the aid of the bank manager.

Then, still disguised as Lloyd George, he walked into the room where they had placed Andrew the night before.

Andrew jumped up at the sight of his old P.M.

"What are you doing here, sir?" Andrew asked as he offered "Lloyd George" his chair.

"Andrew, though I am no longer Prime Minister, I am not without special assignments from Mr. Baldwin. In this instance, it may have to do with a certain investigation concerning illegal shipments of alcohol."

"Of course, sir; I understand fully."

"And that's the point, Andrew. The investigation is over and you shan't speak of it again."

"I understand, sir. I was wondering why nothing had happened after my reports were filed."

"Let's just say that this particular group of men have a particular use for us. And we do not want that use disturbed."

"I understand, sir."

"Oh, and one other thing before I leave and you're set free. That order I had given a few years ago concerning Dr. Watson..."

"Yes?"

"That order is rescinded. He is not to be harmed in any manner. Understood?"

"Of course, sir, of course."

"Good, good. You're free to leave now, Andrew. And Andrew, I promise to put in a very good word to your direct superior. Good luck."

With that, Andrew left, never to return. But what intrigued Holmes was how
easily Andrew accepted the fact that David Lloyd George had even visited him in that room.

In preparation for this encounter, Holmes, as Mr. Stash, had sent word to Andrew's superior to be sure Andrew would be assigned something farther away from London; perhaps somewhere in the Punjab. The superior was just another in a long line of civil servants with whom Mr. Stash had become, shall we say, friendly.

Holmes now doffed Lloyd George, carefully replaced false facial hair to match what he had shaved, and as Mr. Stash once again, returned to Lloyd George.

"You will forgive me, sir, for any discomfort. But you are now free to go. However, while no physical harm has come to you because you cooperated, I cannot guarantee what might happen if you discuss last night. Although as you are aware, it is best that you remain healthy and safe. Do we have an understanding?"

"Yes, yes, we have an understanding. Now how will I leave?

"I'm terribly sorry, but you must be blindfolded again. You'll be driven safely to within a very short distance of your home. I wish you good luck."

Lloyd George was home presently and still safe in the knowledge that no harm would come to him, thereby insuring my safety. But totally unaware of what would soon befall him.

But Holmes, as yet, did not know who Yrjö was.

Reilly And Bugsy

On the morning of August 29, 1923, Bugsy Siegel walked alone out of Lindy's on Broadway in Manhattan, one of the most popular meeting places for anyone who was anyone, no matter how you got to be anyone, and he stopped short. There, in front of him, leaning against a cab, was Reilly.

"What the...? Jesus you got some way of poppin' up. What the hell you doin' here, Moo?" Moo was that nickname Siegel had given Reilly in London. "How the hell did ya find me?"

"Why, Ben. Who in New York doesn't know about Mr. Benjamin Siegel? And that he visits Lindy's every morning for breakfast?"

Siegel extended his hand, "Yeah, you're right on the money."

Reilly opened the cab door and gestured for Siegel to get in.

"Ya tryin' t' take me for a ride?" Siegel laughed, as he got into the cab.

Once seated in the rear, Reilly spoke.

"Exactly, Ben, but not in the way you mean. What I have to discuss with you could very well cost Katherine and her family their lives."

"What family? She told me they were croaked."

"To a degree, that's correct. Ben, where can we go where it's private and we can talk. Just tell the driver."

"Take us to 725 Seventh, it's only a few blocks down," Siegel said to the driver. "I got an office up there," he said to Reilly.

It took only five minutes to arrive at the building and Siegel and Reilly rode up to the seventh floor where Siegel proudly showed Reilly the front door of his office, which was nothing more than frosted glass on the top, wood on the bottom. But there were gold letters on the frosted glass. The first line read: "Mr. Benjamin J. Siegel". Directly underneath: "Proprietor".

Siegel stood there with Reilly for a moment, just looking at the gold letters, as Reilly saw the pride in Siegel's face.

"Very, very nice, Ben. But proprietor of what, precisely?"

"What ever the hell I want," Siegel answered as the unlocked the door and the men went in.

The room was completely bare except for one small desk, one chair in front, one in back, a table to the rear of the desk, on which various forms of alcohol were placed, with glasses to the side. There was also a Murphy bed.

Siegel saw the puzzled look on Reilly's face as he looked around and said, "Yeah, it ain't much, but I call it home. That Murphy bed gets a hell of a lot a use.

"This ain't got nothin' t' do with Meyer or Charlie or any of the guys. Sometimes I need to be alone. And sometimes I need to be alone with a dame. So siddown and tell me what the hell is so secret, Moo," Siegel said as he sat behind the desk with Reilly in front. They both leaned towards each other.

"Ben, if you love Katherine, no one must know what I'm about to tell you. You may not believe it, but no one is to know. Not Meyer, not Charlie, no one. As I said, it can cost Katherine her life."

"Jesus, what the hell are you gonna tell me?"

With that, Reilly proceeded to tell the truth about Olga and her family. But nothing of Holmes or Watson's involvement, at all. Most importantly, if Siegel were to marry Olga, the scrutiny about the new Mrs. Siegel could lead to the disclosure of who she is, where the remaining Romanovs were, and more attempted murders by the Bolsheviks.

Siegel sat there with his mouth open and his blue eyes so wide that they resembled two large circular swimming pools.

"Olga? Her real name is Olga? Hey, I love Katherine, Olga or whatever she calls herself. But her father, that anti-semitic idiot, I oughta kill him myself."

Reilly was now speaking to Siegel the way Lansky spoke to him. Very calmly.

"Ben, that wouldn't be a good idea. Remember, I'm a Russian Jew and I married Olga's sister. She knows who you are and what you do; it would be easy for you to tell her that you're not going to marry her because it's too dangerous. That she could wind up dead in another one of your gang wars.

"She could understand that, Ben. Sure it would hurt her, maybe for a long time, but getting murdered and having your family murdered will hurt a lot more. After all she's been through, she just doesn't deserve anymore anguish."

Siegel was quite for a very long time as he sat with his head down, in his hands, shaking from side to side. Then he said, "But I could protect her. I got enough guys to be with her every minute of every day. She would be safe."

"Ben, not to be flip about this, but your Presidents Lincoln and Garfield were protected, too; and they were assassinated. If two presidents could be killed like that, you have no guarantee for Olga. Ben, for once, really do the right thing."

Finally and reluctantly, Siegel agreed. But he would tell her tomorrow. Tonight, they had plans to have fun up at the Cotton Club with Meyer and his wife, Anne, and Charlie and one of his girls. He would have one last happy night with her and tell her in the morning.

Reilly, relieved, suggested they both have a drink. Siegel agreed and did the honours.

"What's the Cotton Club?" Reilly asked.

Siegel shrugged and shook his head at this tourist.

"Only the hottest jazz joint in the country. It's up in Harlem. Run by one of our guys, Owney Madden. In fact, the guy's a limey, like you. Say, why don't you come up with me tonight. Owney would love meetin' another limey."

"I don't think that's a very good idea, Ben. What if Olga sees me? She might suspect something."

"It's a very good idea and she won't see ya. I'll have Owney put ya at a table with Meyer and Charlie way across the room from me and Katherine. Meyer and Charlie know about ya' already from what I told them when I got back. Katherine will never see ya."

"You told your friends about what happened in London?" Reilly asked.

"I tell Meyer and Charlie everythin'," Siegel said, then saw the consternation in Reilly's eyes.

"Don't worry, Moo. I know this is one thing I can't tell 'em, for Katherine's sake. But, hey, they laughed like crazy when I told 'em about me holdin' a gat on you while you was holdin' a gat on that Georgie guy who was holdin' a gat on Johnny. They almost pissed their pants they thought it was so funny. And they loved what you did to that other guy."

"I don't know, Ben, about joining you tonight."

"I do. And ya know me; I don't take 'no' for an answer from nobody. Especially from somebody I almost killed once." He laughed.

Reilly realized it was senseless to argue.

"In fact," Siegel continued, "since you're in town, you might be able to help Meyer and Charlie and me with a little problem."

"Which is?" Reilly asked.

"We got a problem with two tinhorn punks tryin' t' muscle in on our operation. We been planning to rub 'em out. We got the guys and the guns and Meyer and Charlie worked out a pretty good way t' do it, too.

"But since you was good with a gat yourself and I know what you did with Clay or Holmes or whoever the hell that guy was, I'm thinkin' maybe ya might want in when we make our move."

"Ben, not to be ungrateful for such an astounding opportunity, but remember, I'm a guest in your country and I can't run the risk of anything like littering, or crossing the street in an incorrect manner, or partaking in a mass murder. You understand, of course?"

"Listen, those guys are bums. They already tried to bump off Meyer and me but no dice, we're still breathin'. It's those damned Romano brothers, Carlo and Roberto. Like I said we got it all mapped out."

"But as I said, I believe I'll have to pass on this one," Reilly replied.

"Okay, whatever," said Reilly, leaning back in his chair and giving Reilly a decidedly dyspeptic look, "but just so ya don't pull no disappearin' act on me, I'm takin' ya downstairs to some guys that'll fit ya for a tux."

"A tuxedo; why would I want a tuxedo?"

"Because nobody gets into the Cotton Club without a tux. Except the dames. And even some of them wear 'em, too; if you get my drift."

Siegel and Reilly began the ride down the elevator and Reilly wondered just how far downhill this night might go.

The Cotton Club, I

It was the twenty-ninth of August and having finished my last lecture in New York at about eight P.M, and before we embarked home the next day, I had planned a little surprise for Elizabeth.

I had read in the Times, the New York Times, that is, about a sensational new hot jazz club in Harlem called The Cotton Club. Not that Elizabeth and I were, at all, jazz aficionados; but the article had mentioned that famous entertainers and sports figures and politicians would attend every night, and you just never knew who might suddenly be seated at the table next to yours.

When I told Elizabeth my surprise, she thought it a wonderful idea. We changed into formal attire and had a cab at the front of the hotel take us up to Harlem about ten.

When the driver asked "where to?" and I said "I believe 142nd Street and Lenox Avenue, he brightened and said, "Oh, you're going up to The Cotton Club. Ha-cha-cha-cha!" and he took off at a rather alarming rate of speed, providing a running commentary as he careened through the still busy streets of Manhattan.

"Hey, I hear everyone has a hot time up there. Yeah, you got gangsters mixin' wit' movie stars, mixin' wit' baseball players and Owney Madden keeps everyone in line."

"I'm sorry, just who is this Owney Madden?"

"Ya kiddin' me? You ain't never heard of Owney Madden?"

"I'm sorry, but we're not from around here. We're from England."

"No kiddin'. Then you must know Madden."

"I'm sorry, but I don't understand."

"Madden's a limey, too, so I figure you gotta know him."

"No, my friend, the United Kingdom is quite large and I'm sure that I don't know Mr. Madden."

That seemed to disappoint the driver to such an extent that for the balance of the ride he remained gruffly silent, shoulders hunched, hands tight upon the wheel and eyes fixed firmly upon the road flying beneath us.

Presently we were there and from where I sat in the cab, it appeared as though everything I had read was going to prove true; such were the lights and the crush of people outside.

It seemed as though all of Harlem was lit by the capital letters spelling out COTTON CLUB, each letter as high as our cab.

I got out of the cab first and saw that there were lines stretching for what seemed blocks and my first inclination was to tell Elizabeth not to get out and that we should return to the hotel. But the look on her face had such a childish happiness and anticipation about the lights and the excitement and the sheer electricity of the environment that I hadn't the heart to suggest it.

Instead, I helped her out of the cab and as we began walking to find the end of that limitless line, I casually remarked, "Perhaps we should have worn our hiking shoes. I fear this line may stretch back to Piccadilly."

Elizabeth laughed, but then we heard a man with a Liverpudlian accent say, "Did I hear someone just mention Piccadilly?"

Elizabeth and I turned to see a fireplug of a man who appeared to be in his early thirties, smiling broadly before us.

"Why, yes. I was trying to make jest of this interminable line."

"What line? I don't see no line? Follow me."

Elizabeth and I looked at each other, shrugged as we smiled and followed the man to the club's entrance. Once there the Art Deco style brass double doors were opened by two large and threatening gatekeepers and we heard, "Good evening, Mr. Madden", "How are you tonight, Mr. Madden." It seemed that Owney Madden, himself, was our escort.

As we walked into the interior, we couldn't, as yet, see the stage, but we could hear the music, smell cigarette and rich cigar smoke mingled with other indulgent aromas and we marveled at the accumulation of glittering jewelry and impeccably dressed men and women, all in formal attire.

"So how d'ya like my place?" asked Madden.

"Why, it's nothing short of marvelous," Elizabeth said with an admiring chuckle.

"Yeah, I think so, too," Madden said, smilling.

At that, he crooked his finger at a maître d' and told him, "These people here are special friends of mine. Take 'em to the best table in the house and if any of the guys come by and want that table, you just tell 'em that Owney wants these friends there, got it? And anything they want is one the house? Ya got that, too?"

"Yes, Mr. Madden. Of course, Mr. Madden."

"Why, Mr. Madden, we couldn't," said Elizabeth, but Madden cut her off.

"Please, lady. It's my pleasure just to hear the two of you talk. Say, I must be so rude; what are your names and where are you from?"

I said, "This is my wife, Elizabeth, and I'm Dr. John Watson. We're from London?"

As soon as I completed my sentence I thought he was going mad.

"Dr. Watson? Dr. Watson? The Sherlock Holmes Dr. Watson?"

Sheepishly, I concurred.

"Well, goddamn it, I read every one of them stories of yours. I figure if I could pick up some thinkin' tips from that Holmes guy it might help me in what I do."

"Mr. Madden, from the looks of this magnificent club of yours, I don't believe you need any help from my chronicles."

"Hey, don't knock yourself, doctor. And I'm real sorry about the Krauts killing your friend. He was a true Englishman, doing what he was doing for his country, and all."

"Yes, well, he's sorely missed," I said.

"Okay, so just follow that guy waiting for you and he'll take you to your table. But Dr. Watson, later, I want you to sign one of your stories that I got up in my office; okay?" It seemed a command as well as a request and I, of course said I'd be happy to repay his kindness in any way I could.

With that, the maître d' showed us to our table which was right in the centre of the room, directly in front of the raised stage. As we sat, the band was playing some very rapid piece, and people on either side craned their necks to see who we were to receive such regal seating.

Elizabeth and I quietly smiled at each other as we saw the heads being put together and tongues wagging, obviously asking the other tongues if they could identify us.

Then Elizabeth nudged me, and put her head next to mine. "Don't look now, but at the table to the right, I think, it's Al Jolson." And so it was.

I had craned my own neck so spectacularly to see him that the girl he was with nudged him in my direction. Jolson turned, saw me staring at him as if he were a baboon in a tuxedo and said, "Hey, pal, you're getting to look at my pretty kisser for nothing. You oughta come up to the Wintergarden and pay for the privilege."

I straightened my neck back to its natural position as Elizabeth laughed at my discomfort and a magnum of champagne was brought to the table and served. This really seemed to pique Jolson's interest.

He yelled over to us, "Hey, just who are you two? Owney don't even treat me that well."

I don't know from where it came, but I looked squarely at Mr. Jolson and said in the most snooty tone you could imagine, "Sir, I am the Duke of Walsingham and the third in line to the British throne."

"Well holy mackerel, Dukiepoo. Your cousin is about to begin."

As he said that, the lights went down and none other than Duke Ellington and his orchestra began to play. He was to later gain world fame because of the Cotton Club, but Elizabeth and I were nothing short of mesmorised. We had never known such kinetic rhythms and melodic orchestrations.

Even at our age, we found ourselves tapping our feet and swaying in our seats.

Jolson yelled over again, "Now ya got it Dukiepoo! Now ya got it!"

This was most certainly not Gilbert and Sullivan.

The Cotton Club, II

It was about almost eleven when Siegel and Reilly arrived at the Cotton Club. Olga had been escorted to the club earlier by Lansky and Anne. Siegel took Reilly in through a special side entrance where the guards greeted the two with, "Hello, Mr. Siegel," "Have a great time, Mr. Siegel," but looked very carefully at Reilly.

"Relax, guys; he's with me," Siegel said.

Which drew the additional, "Of course, Mr. Siegel," "No problem, Mr. Siegel."

Reilly and Siegel continued down a hallway till a guard opened another door and suddenly they were in the main entrance room. People were greeting Siegel left and right, but Reilly, though nervous about his meeting with Olga, was taking a moment to just drink in the atmosphere, as Elizabeth and I had done.

Siegel then nudged him and pointed to the table where Olga was sitting with the awaiting party.

"I'll be over in a minute; I gotta talk to Owney upstairs in his office. You go and introduce yourself."

"But, Ben, you said I wouldn't have to see Olga. I think I'd better leave."

Siegel hardened.

"You ain't goin' nowhere, Moo. Just go over there. Meyer and Charlie know you're comin'. But Katherine doesn't, so don't give her a heart attack."

There was no reasoning with someone like Siegel. He hadn't earned his nickname, Bugsy, for nothing. And if he didn't do what Siegel wanted, there was no telling what Siegel would, in fact, do. So Reilly decided to do as instructed and rely on his wit to bring resolve to this new problem.

As Reilly made his way through the teeming tables packed so tightly together, trying not to bump into anyone, he stopped dead; for now he literally faced a another new problem: me. I was coming straight toward him on my way to use the loo.

Then I spied him, as well, and likewise stood frozen. If one such shock were not enough to my system, Reilly first nodded to say nothing, which I was not capable of doing in any event, then moved his head to the left, in the direction of a certain table.

My second great shock came as I followed his nod and saw Olga seated there. I do not believe that even in all my years as Holmes' confidant and compatriot in all I had chronicled, had I ever been so utterly dumbfounded and at a loss of what to do next. It was Reilly who gave me direction.

He moved his head backwards indicating that I should continue on without any recognition, and since I was, at the moment, in need of the loo to an imperative degree, that is precisely what I did.

Reilly then walked over to the table where Olga sat with the Lanskys and Luciano and his girl. They looked cautiously up at Reilly, and Olga looked up to see him, as well. She gave a gasp as Reilly signaled by slightly shaking his head not to recognise him, as he had just done with me.

But Olga was a Romanov Grand Duchess, and had the training and bearing to conduct herself properly under any circumstances; as she had so nobly demonstrated in Russia.

"Gentlemen, I believe you're expecting me?" Reilly asked gallantly as he bowed his head slightly in gentlemanly gesture to the women.

It was Meyer who spoke first. "Hey, yeah. You're that Reilly guy. That English friend of Benny's. With the gats and all."

"I admit it."

"Siddown, siddown," Luciano said. We got chairs saved for you and Ben. Where is he?"

"He'll be along in a minute. I believe he was speaking with Mr. Madden in his office."

"Oh, yeah," Lansky said. As Reilly still stood, Meyer introduced him to his wife, to Charlie, and Charlie's girl for the night, Lucille. Charlie's girls never had last names.

"And last but not least, Katherine Kasey, Benny's girl. She's English, too. Like Charlie said, siddown. Here next to Katherine. Katherine Kasey meet Reilly, uh, what is your first name, anyway?"

"Sidney, it's Sidney."

As Reilly sat next to Olga and she extended her hand for him to shake, she kept a steady, yet inquisitive gaze at him and betrayed nothing.

Reilly thought it best if he cued Olga.

"It's a pleasure to meet you, Katherine. Ben has told me so much about you."

"I should hope so, Mr. Reilly, though Ben hasn't mentioned you to me, at all."

"I guess I'm just not very important."

What happened in the next few minutes happened while I was still otherwise occupied.

240

I heard rapid arms fire, like machine guns; then tables overturning, women screaming, the sound of people running; in short, collective chaos. All I could think of was Elizabeth and that I had to get to her.

I ran outside to be greeted with the sour scent of gunpowder and the sight of men and women, wounded and dead. I fought my way, as best I could, against the mass of people trying to push passed me on their flight to the exits, then I saw Elizabeth in the midst of that mass.

Somehow, she fought her way free, ran into my arms and I shielded her against the bodies slamming into us both. I managed to steer us to an enclave protected by a thin wall. I held her there and we watched the frenzied surge to the outside. Then I felt someone tap me. It was Reilly. I had completely forgotten about him in my worry for Elizabeth.

"Dr. Watson, please, come with me. I need you."

Elizabeth looked at him, then me with puzzlement, faintly remembering him from his visit to our home; but I whispered to her, "It's all right Elizabeth. This man is a great friend. Come with me, I don't want to leave you here alone."

Reilly took us to the table he had indicated earlier. The table was overturned. The men and two of the women seemed to be unwounded, but then I looked down and saw that Olga lay there. I kneeled immediately and though I examined her as thoroughly as possible, I almost immediately knew she was dead.

I began to cry and Elizabeth put her arms on my shoulders and lifted me up, her eyes questioning why I was crying. But there was no time to answer.

Suddenly Siegel and Madden and some of his men were by our side. It was Siegel's turn to kneel by Olga; whom he took in his arms and began rocking back and forth; weeping like a little boy. I had no idea who he was, of course, but understood immediately the delicate connection there.

Lansky stood holding Anne, Luciano the same with Lucille. Presently they let them go and walked over to Madden, who asked, "Who?"

"The Romanos," Charlie said.

"The crazy dagos. Everyone knows this club is off-limits," Madden said. Then he continued, "Charlie, Meyer, the cops'll be here soon. Best to get out the private way. You better go now."

Siegel, still weeping, looked up at the only other person he truly loved, Lansky, and Lansky looked down at the man he loved as a little brother.

"Benny, we'll get 'em for this. We'll get 'em," Lansky said softly. Luciano was nodding in assurance.

Siegel, still holding Olga then heard Reilly say softly, as well, "Ben, the problem you mentioned before. This is now mine as well as yours. We're doing this together."

Only Siegel knew what he meant and why.

"Okay, Moo," he said, "just me and you."

Lansky and Luciano looked at each other not understanding but wisely remaining mute.

"Benny, we have to leave. Some of Owney's men will help with Katherine if you want. We'll take care of her proper," Lansky said.

Siegel nodded agreement, stood, but took Olga in his arms and carried her out as Madden's men cleared the way;

Lansky, Anne, Luciano, Lucille, Reilly, Elizabeth and I following.

I was holding Elizabeth again as we followed, she looking at me for any form of explanation, as she, too, wept at the death of the beautiful young woman. I calmed her as much as I was able, but I knew that I since I could tell her nothing of the facts behind my relationship with Reilly, I would have to invent something she might believe.

When we got outside, Reilly gestured for me and Elizabeth to get into one of the waiting autos, which we did; and which took us to our hotel. Then, halfway back, I realized that I hadn't told Reilly where Elizabeth and I were staying, but further realized that since we'd be leaving for England later in the day, it didn't much matter. He knew where we lived in London.

All I could do was silently pray for his safety.

Home In London, A Burial In New York

While aboard *Olympic* once again, sailing for home, Elizabeth and I spent the next few days trying to forget the heartbreaking events of which we had been part; and which, of course, was not humanly possible. We reached home on the fourth of September.

The tale I concocted as explanation of my relationship with Reilly was thin, to say the least, and Elizabeth saw through it immediately.

"Reilly was with you in Afghanistan? He saved your life when a crazed Afghani tribesman was about to cut your head off? John, puh-lease. That man called you Dr. Watson; not John, as he would've if you two had served together and he had saved your life."

I thought it plausible; though. Elizabeth knew of my service there, so why not have me saved by Reilly? But then again, I could not change the fact of how Reilly had addressed me and, by heavens, Elizabeth was thinking like Holmes.

From this I learned one great lesson, which is never too late to learn: one can never fool a wife who is thinking like Holmes. Or simply thinking as a wife.

While Elizabeth and I voyaged homeward, Reilly and Siegel had begun planning how to exact revenge. But there were more delicate matters to be settled immediately.

First, Siegel paid a Russian Orthodox priest a hefty sum, combined with an ominous warning, not to not ask any questions and perform the proper burial ceremony for Olga.

She was buried in the Holy Trinity Russian Orthodox Cemetery directly north of New York City, in a small town called Yonkers. Lansky and Luciano were there at the burial alongside Siegel and Reilly.

The headstone Siegel ordered to be placed there bore this name: Katherine Siegel.

Later, when Lansky and Luciano asked Siegel what was going on with him and Reilly and why he wanted only Reilly along to tend to the Romanos, Siegel simply said, "Meyer, Charlie, you just gotta trust me on this. This guy, Reilly, played a very special part in Katherine's life, kinda like an uncle, and this is something we gotta do together. We can do it and we gotta do it."

Lansky and Luciano, knowing Siegel so well, simply shrugged.

"Go do what ya gotta do," Lansky said. "Gay mit mazel, boychik." Yiddish for "good luck, little boy."

"Ditto," Luciano said. But if you need anything, anything, you know we got your back."

By the time Elizabeth and I were safely back in our home, Siegel and Reilly had done what they had to do.

Reilly and Bugsy's Revenge

In Olga's and Ben's flat, it was Reilly who devised the specifics of the plan, to which Siegel agreed. The night before it was put into action, as they went over every contingency and believed all unforeseen occurrences had been considered, they rested over some brandy. The only outside help Reilly needed was a driver who knew the streets of Manhattan and Brooklyn. Reles would drive.

"Ben, you know that once we meet with Meyer and Charlie to confirm that everything went well, I'll be gone. I'll be going back to the island. We'll never see each other again."

"Yeah, I know the game. I woulda loved for ya to hang around here and join Meyer and Charlie and me, but I got ya." Then he added, "Reilly, I wanna thank you, too. You were a true friend to Katherine. And you were doing the right thing. Thank God I never got the chance to break up with her, because to tell ya the truth, I don't think I woulda been able t' do it."

"Charlie always says domani," Siegel said. "But with me and you, it's 'morgn'." This is the Yiddish equivalent of domani; tomorrow.

They clinked glasses.

Carlo Romano lived on Ryder Street in an Italian section of Brooklyn. It was a row house and the fathers of the families that lived on either side were part of his gang. By living in the middle of these men, Romano felt he had added protection. And he was correct in that assumption. Which is why Reilly planned to execute him when he was not guarded in that manner.

It was the third of September, about seven a.m. Romano was being driven to his garlic import company office in downtown Brooklyn, on Nevins Street. As his auto pulled up to his office, he saw a delivery truck from the Giovanni Garlic Company parked outside and a delivery man in company coveralls leaning leisurely against the truck. There was another behind the wheel.

As Romano got out of his auto he said, "Hey, youse guys are here real early. You got some good garlic for me?"

"Great stuff," Reilly said as went closer to Romano, pulled a revolver from his coverall pocket and put a bullet directly into Romano's head. Then, as Romano's driver got out, he too, was shot by Reilly.

Reilly looked down at Romano, put two more rounds into his head and spit on his body. He then went around to check the driver, and though he saw he was dead, put a round into the man's head for good measure. Then he got back into the truck and Reles drove them away.

At the same time, in Little Italy in downtown Manhattan, Roberto Romano lay asleep in his flat. Siegel stood over him with a can of petrol. The guard at the door had already been dispatched.

Romano was awakened by the petrol being poured all over his body. Then Reilly whispered, "This is for Olga," dropped a match and ran from the room.

Two hours later, Siegel calmly walked into a private office where Lansky, Luciano and Reilly were waiting and drinking.

"Fachtik?" Lansky asked. Yiddish for "finished?"

"In spades," Siegel replied. Then he looked at Reilly who gave a simple nod.

Siegel sat between Lansky and Luciano as Lansky poured him a drink.

"Ya know, Moo, I been talkin' with Meyer and Charlie and we'd really like ya to hang around here. You're like one of us."

"Yeah," Luciano said, "we could use a guy like you." Lansky nodded affirmatively.

"Gentlemen, I'm afraid that just wouldn't do. Ben understands and I hope you will, too. Now that everything is done, I have to leave. There's a boat waiting," Reilly said. "But I'm sorry that I'm leaving you to face the music."

"What music?" Lansky asked. Nobody saw nothin' and we're used to takin' the heat anyways."

Lansky and Luciano both wished him well and hugged him goodbye, still expressing regret at his decision.

Siegel hugged him and whispered in his ear, "Thanks, again, Moo. I'll never forget you."

As Reilly was closing the door behind him, he saw Lansky and Luciano patting Siegel reassuringly on the shoulders, and he heard them talking about what to do next with their growing criminal network.

Reilly Returns To Tatiana

Reilly had planned it so that he'd be able to board a boat to the Bahamas in a very few hours after the Romano matter had been settled. He would, hopefully, be gone before the tabloids had even reported the latest gangland outrage.

That was the easy part. The most difficult part would be telling Tatiana and the Tsar what had happened to Olga. And then Marie and Anastasia, if she could be located.
From Nassau, he notified Tatiana when he'd be returning and dreaded his reunion.

. As it transpired, he would be back in Eleuthera one day after Elizabeth and I had arrived back in London.

As the skiff hit the little dock at the compound, Tatiana was there to greet him, holding Alix, with little Sidney, at her side. The Tsar was there, as well, standing next to Funny Oscar, who had come to help Reilly with his luggage.

From the false smile on his face, Tatiana knew immediately something was terribly wrong, but said nothing until they were back at the house and alone in their room, her father below, playing with the children.

"Tell me, Sidney. Be honest. Olga?"

"Tatiana, there is no way for me soften this, Olga is dead."

Tatiana didn't cry, she simply said, "I already knew it, I felt it. Before you even left I knew that this would be one problem you wouldn't be able to bring to a happy solution. How? Tell me everything."

Not wanting to have Tatiana or the Tsar haunted by the truth of Olga's death, he simply said that she had become ill, pneumonia, and had perished with him at her side. He also assured her of Olga's strict Orthodox burial, which, he knew, would ease her mind, however marginally.

He told her that the young man who loved Olga and who she loved, had been devastated by the tragedy and had been with Reilly at her bedside and at the burial.

Tatiana resolved that it would be she alone to give the news to her father.

"Sidney, go to the children, they've missed you so frightfully since you've been gone. Take them outside, I don't want them to see their grandfather so distraught."

With that, Reilly gathered the children and Tatiana went to speak with her father.

Outside with Sidney and Alix, Reilly saw Funny Oscar and called him over.

"Funny Oscar, I know I've said this to you many times, but thank you for everything you've done for my family. I was able to do what I had to do knowing they'd be safe because of you."

"They've become my family, too," Funny Oscar said.

"They most assuredly have, haven't they? But Funny Oscar, what about your own family? Do you have one? I should have asked you about this long ago."

"Don't worry yourself about it. I have no family anymore, other than yours. Mine have long ago since passed on. Sickness. Accidents. The war. I don't dwell on it."

"Then you're still SIS?"

Funny Oscar shrugged coyly, then said, "I was here already. I like it here. It's warmer than Kent. As you know, mates at SIS will always report in from time to time."

"Yes, I'm only too aware of that," Reilly said.

It was Yrjö who was to prove that statement so true.

When Tatiana came to Reilly after speaking with her father, she was doubly spent. Reilly left the children with Funny Oscar as he took Tatiana to that same bench on which they sat when he first arrived at Winding Bay.

"Tatiana....:

"She cut him off. I know, I know. But please just stay and rest for a little while. The children need you, I need you, and you need us. Just rest a little and then go and finish this business.

"I know you'll let Marie know what's happened. And Sidney, if there's any way for you to find Anastasia; I know you'll find it."

He simply nodded, put his arm around her, and they sat quietly, looking out at the cobalt Caribbean.

Reilly In London, II

After heeding Tatiana and taking that little while to rest and be with his family, Reilly was back in London on October 31, All Hallows Eve. How fitting. His passport still showed him as Roland Windsor.

His first task was to contact Marie. He accomplished this by the simple expediency of waiting outside her home the next day and then walking behind her as she made her way for errands of the day.

He walked up to her right side, but not so close to give her pause, took a few steps past her at a faster pace, then turned to his left so she could see who he was. Of course, she stopped dead.

"Just continue walking and don't say anything." This she did, but only haltingly, trying to catch her breath.

"No one is following us. But I must speak to you. Come closer so it'll just look like two mates strolling and talking. We'll sit on that bench over there, in that park." He indicated a bench not far away. Once seated, he began to speak.

"Marie, I'm happy to see you're well. And I trust William is?"

"Reilly, yes, yes, we're both very well."

"Marie your father, Tatiana and the children are all well, too." Marie saw the hesitancy in Reilly and asked, "Reilly, I know there's something wrong. What is it?"

"Marie, Olga has passed on."

She didn't cry but could not understand.

"But how? She was young and healthy; how did it happen?"

As with Tatiana, there was no need to have Marie learn the true nature of Olga's death, so he had to dissemble once again.

"I was there with her, Marie, if that's any consolation. She just became ill. Very ill with pneumonia. The doctors tried, but she slipped away." He then told her about the Russian Orthodox burial, as well.

"That is good, then. My big sister, the one who was always looking out for me. I still remember when I was such a little girl, how she would chase away my lady servant who was trying to dress my hair, so that she could do it instead.

"She would take the brush and so slowly and lovingly just brush out my hair and go over and over and say in her own little girl voice, 'See, Marie. See how beautiful you are and your hair is? And I'll always be here. I'll always be here.' It's funny what you remember."

Reilly said nothing; just listened. But for a long while, Marie remained silent. Then, as if she were weighing the good and the bad of things, she turned to Reilly and asked, "Now tell me, and tell me truly, how are my niece and nephew? For I suspect I'll never see them."

Suddenly, he realized he had never been asked about his children before and he had the new sensation of the beaming father bragging about his offspring; a sensation he thoroughly enjoyed.

Then he remembered. He stood and pulled a tiny photo of the children from his wallet and put it into Marie's hands as if he was presenting her a crown jewel. Which, in a way, he was.

"Alix and Sidney," Reilly said.

"Oh, they're so beautiful," Marie said. Then she began to cry.

Reilly tried to jest, "Of course, they look like their mother; thank heavens. They both have her beautiful, slightly Asiatic eyes.

"Marie, Marie, I wish you could hold them. Sidney is rambunctious and obstinate and playful and smart and…"

Marie was now laughing as she said, "Reilly, there's no need to recite every happy adjective in the English language. I understand."

"And Alix, she's just the sweetest little package you can imagine," Reilly added.

Marie sat back a bit from Reilly, as if examining a transformation and said, "Look at you, just look at you."

"Must I?" Reilly asked.

"You are a totally different man than the one who shepherded us through Russia. You're happy."

He grew pensive, then said quietly, "Yes, I am happy. For the first time in my life I am truly happy. But I'm not a changed man. Leopards cannot lose their spots. It's the nature of the beast.

"I'm sorry that I couldn't bring a photo of Tatiana or the Tsar; but you know why."

"Reilly, what about William? Can I tell him you're here?"

"Not right now; there's no need for that and it may only confuse things."

"What things?"

"You know better than to ask that of me?"

"You're right. But there's something I must ask of you." Reilly nodded to proceed.

"Anastasia. You know she's disappeared and I've tried, but I can't find out what's happened. I'm very, very worried. I don't want to lose another sister; my baby sister."

"Tatiana asked me, too. I'll try to find her; but I have some other business which I must attend to first."

"I understand. Will I see you again before you leave England?"

"Who can say? I've always felt like a leaf in the wind. Right now, I'm not sure which way the wind is blowing."

Now, it was Marie who grew pensive.

"What is it?" Reilly asked.

"I don't know if this means anything, but I've had the funniest feeling, from time to time, that I've been followed. I mentioned this to William and he even took to hiding about to see if I was being followed, but he couldn't find anyone."

"I see. And how long did you have this feeling?"

"Oddly enough, from just about the time I arrived in London. Silly, I suppose."

"And when did you stop feeling as if you were being followed?"

"After our return from our honeymoon."

Suddenly, Reilly's demeanor changed radically and he smiled.

"Marie, I may be able to find out where Anastasia is much easier than I had supposed."

"But how? How could that be possible from the few words I've just said?"

"I can't divulge that now. We must leave it at that."

Reilly thought to himself, "Holmes."

An Appeal To Holmes

It was an easy enough thread for Reilly to tie together.

Marie had felt followed from when she arrived in London, when she was most vulnerable, then no longer after her marriage to William.

Believing that however bizarre Holmes may have become, he may still have felt an overweening responsibility for the safety of Marie and Anastasia; so he had them followed to prevent anything untoward.

And if he knew where Marie lived, it was only natural that he would also know where Anastasia had gotten to. So Reilly made his way to that corner of Varrance and Lomas the next morning.

He was, of course, stopped at the front door by the same men he had met on his previous visit. One man went up to Mr. Stash to see what should be done.

When the man returned, he motioned for Reilly to follow him. This Reilly did and entered Holmes' office.

Holmes, as Mr. Stash, facial hair now regrown, sat in his chair, his body tilted towards Reilly as if poised to strike and motioned Reilly to sit opposite him.

"Why have you come to see me this time?" Holmes asked.

"Holmes, I need your help."

"Why?"

"Because I believe you're the only man who can help me. Holmes, I need to find Anastasia."

"Why?"

"Because the family is worried sick. She's disappeared. And there's another reason, as well."

Holmes indicated, again with a gesture of his head, for Reilly to continue.

"Holmes, Olga is dead."

Holmes recoiled as if slapped in the face. It appeared he had not received the news from his American colleagues.

"How? When?"

Reilly told him everything that happened in New York and he could see it pained Holmes deeply; even as Mr. Stash. But Reilly wondered why the men in New York hadn't told him. Then he remmbered they knew nothing about the connection between Olga and Holmes.

"Holmes, I know you followed Marie…"

Holmes cut him off. "How did you know that?"

Reilly explained, then continued, "I thought you might have had Anastasia followed for protection, as well. And if that was true, you'd know where she is. But I have no idea of how you could've discovered that they were here."

Holmes seemed pleased at that and told Reilly of how he tracked them. Then he wrote something on a piece of paper and passed it across the desk to Reilly.

"Paris? Anastasia is in Paris?"

"Obviously. What will you do once you've found her?"

"I promised the Tsar and Tatiana that I'd try to bring her back to Eleuthera where she can be cared for. Barring that, I'm just not sure and will cross that bridge when I come to it."

"Then go cross your bridge."

Reilly decided to ask a question, though he suspected it would bring ire.

"Holmes, please forgive me, but for all that you mean to my family, to Watson, and to me, as well, why do you persist with this masquerade?"

"Because it is easier," Holmes said quietly.

"I don't understand. All you have to do is cast off this disguise and re-emerge as yourself."

"You think I have not considered that, Reilly?" What about Watson? I have not been able to discover who the other special branch agent is that can take his life if I resurface. And are there more I have not been made aware of?

"There is also a certain pleasure I've discovered in donning an opponent's mantle. It is perverse, but it is also gratifying." As Holmes said this, he was rubbing his hands along the sides of his unkempt suit; his fingers fondling the fabric as he did so.

Reilly watched these actions and could not reconcile the image of the Holmes he knew in Russia and the man who sat across the desk. He thought it best not to press the matter.

Then Holmes asked a question that took Reilly aback.

"Reilly, haven't you, who has spent your life donning and doffing various personas, ever thought of becoming someone like me?"

"I don't understand," Reilly answered, quite truthfully.

"What I am suggesting is that since you are intimately acquainted with our friends in New York and what I have accomplished since becoming Clay, perhaps you might like to step into my shoes as I step down."

Reilly thought Holmes totally mad, at this point. Holmes saw the look on Reilly's face and continued.

"Reilly, think of what you would be able to offer Tatiana and the children in material wealth. You would be returning to Tatiana all the luxury so sadistically snatched from her by the Bolsheviks. You would simply be returning what was rightfully hers."

Reilly, at first, could not speak; so bizarre were Holmes' words.

"You can't mean any of that," Reilly finally said.

"I most certainly do. You are the only person I know, other than Meyer, who can combine brains with brutality. I am not getting any younger, Reilly, and I would like to pass on what I've built to someone I can trust. Someone who will be able to take what I've built and build it even larger. Someone who can also act as guardian for Watson and his family. And the remaining Romanovs."

"Holmes, that is all too fantastic. I can't even absorb the concept. But for now, I'll take your advice and leave for Paris as soon as possible."

As he was about to leave the office, he turned and asked, "Holmes, is there anything I might be able to do for you, other than what you've just proposed."

Holmes said simply, "You know what that is."

He most certainly did.

A Finnish Friend Returns

The next day, Reilly made it known to the two reaming SIS operatives he felt he could trust, that I was about to break my silence and reveal to the world what I knew. His idea for this latest subterfuge was that my story might be circulated and heard by that unknown agent, causing him to visit me as a warning to remain silent.

Then Reilly would know who he was and how to deal with him. Of course, I knew nothing of this plan nor that Reilly was in London.

Reilly kept a night vigil outside of my home, positive that this person would do as Reilly believed. On the second night, at about eight, Reilly saw a man knock on my door, me open it and let him in.

Since Elizabeth and I usually didn't have callers at this time, Reilly suspected it was time. He came to my front door, opened it, and heard me speaking with a man who sounded strangely familiar. The door to my study was closed, so Reilly could not be sure that he truly recognised the man's voice.

As Reilly had thought, the man was warning me to remain silent or there would be no accounting for what would happen to Holmes.

"But I assure you," I said, "I have no intention of saying anything now or in the future. If my friend is still alive, I cannot risk his safety. But why are you asking me about this after all this time? Is Holmes well? Have you seen him?"

"We heard that you were about to reveal what you knew."

"Now where could you have heard such lies?" I asked.

"From me."

I turned to see Reilly, pistol in hand, standing at the now-opened door.

The man who had a moment before been wondering from where the lies had come, seeing Reilly, simply smiled and said, "Of course."

"Good to see you, Yrjö," Reilly said.

"Likewise," Yrjö, said, "but do you really need to point that pistol?"

"I don't know; do I?"

"Sidney, after all we've meant to each other?" Yrjö seemed to be playfully mocking Reilly.

"You two know each other?" What a foolish question; but it was out of my mouth before I could stop it.

"Yes, yes, Dr. Watson. Sidney and I are old comrades."

"I thought I asked you not to call me that," said Reilly, smiling, as he put his pistol back into his overcoat.

"A mere slip of the tongue."

"Somehow, Yrjö, I don't think anything slips from you," Reilly said.

"How kind of you," Yrjö said.

It was obvious these two men had history, but good or ill?

"Reilly, who is this man? It's obvious you know him."

"Quite well, doctor. But I have no time to waste with our story." I decided to ask no more and to just watch and listen carefully.

So," said Reilly, still smiling at the man, but with a touch of menace in his voice, "it seems you and I have a problem, Yrjö."

"I hadn't noticed."

Now, Reilly's tone grew serious and the smile was gone.

"Enough. We both know why you've come and I'm here to tell you that whatever order you had received from Lloyd George during the war, it's over, done, rescinded, invalid, called off, stopped, cancelled; must I go on?"

"Sidney, I'm very impressed with your knowledge of synonyms, but on whose authority should I cease, desist, etc.?" Yrjö asked, nonchalantly.

"On mine," answered Reilly, smiling again.

"Well, in that case…" Yrjö paused and it was his turn to become serious.

"I'm afraid I'm going to need a better reason."

"How about this: being a Finnish friend."

Yrjö's eyes narrowed. "So you're going to use that now, are you?"

"Anything at my disposal, Yrjö."

Since Reilly had his pistol, the double meaning was quite clear.

"Dr. Watson, I know this is presumptuous of me, but may I ask you to leave your own study so that my friend, here, and I can speak in private?" Reilly asked.

"Under the circumstances, I cannot think of a better alternative," I answered. I left the room, with Yrjö's eyes watching me carefully.

"John, John, who's there," Elizabeth called from upstairs.

"Oh, a slight surprise reunion, you might say/"

"At this hour?"

"Well, I said it was a surprise. I'll be up presently. We're just talking and they'll soon be off."

"Some sort of a reunion that is," she said in brusque finality. I waited outside and then, after about five or so minutes, the door opened and Reilly motioned me back in.

"All is resolved?" I asked.

"Yes, yes," Yrjö said resignedly. "I just wish we Finns weren't such good friends."

With that, he and Reilly hugged, and the man gave me a civilian salute. However, he paused in my study doorway, turned to Reilly and said, "You can best translate it as internal strength; or as you Brits might say, bulldog determination; or as the Yanks might say, not taking crap from anyone."

"Pardon me," Reilly said.

"Sisu," Yrjö said.

"Ah, yes; sisu. Thank you."

"Don't mention it," Yrjö said, as he closed the door and left.

"Sisu?" I asked.

"No matter. Let's just say he owed me one. But you and I have a lot to discuss."

"Yes, why are you here?"

"Dr. Watson, I can trust you because of all we've been through together," Reilly said; not able to tell him of his meeting with Holmes.

"We received some other upsetting news on the island recently, Anastasia has gone missing."

I was confused. I still didn't know how Olga had come to be in New York on that horrid night and now this. Reilly saw my confusion.

"John, I believe I can call you that; there's much I can't explain. But I believe she's in Paris. I'm going to leave as soon as possible. Tatiana has asked, if possible, to bring her back to Eleuthera.

"But I didn't want to be in London without me seeing you again and speaking of what happened in New York."

"Yes, terrible, terrible," I said. "Elizabeth still talks about that poor, beautiful young woman but, of course, she knows nothing of her real identity."

"What happened with Olga was tragic, but it'll serve no purpose for me to elaborate any further; only to let you know she was given a proper burial and I was there.

"What's done is done and all on Eleuthera are well and healthy; Tatiana, the Tsar, Marie. And oh, yes, by the way, there are now two little Reillys on that island."

"Another child?" I asked in total happiness.

"Yes, little Alix. She was born on the seventh of February." With that, Reilly pulled a photo from his wallet to show to me. It was of Alix and little Sidney.

"Oh, Reilly, they are beautiful. Takes after their mother, of course." I laughed.

"I can't argue with you on that point. And now, John, I've got to go. I'm not sure if I'll be able to see you, again, or if I'll be going back directly from France, but in any event, you know you hold the gratitude of all of us."

"I know. Good luck, Reilly. I hope you find her. And if I can help in any way, you know you can depend on me."

"Of course," Reilly said.

With that, he left.

Finding Anastasia

When Reilly stepped out of his hotel about seven the next morning, there was Mr. Stash; albeit one more presentable for public transport.

"What the devil are you doing here?" Reilly asked.

"If you want an answer, thent ask him directly," Holmes replied.

Reilly just shrugged. They proceeded by cab to Victoria Station, then on to Paris by the usual method: rail to Dover Piory, then ferry to Calais, then rail, again, to Paris.

Reilly assumed that perhaps not all of Holmes had dissolved into Clay or this Mr. Stash and that there may still be hope of Holmes becoming Holmes again. After all, Holmes was sitting next to him on an errand of mercy. Though Holmes had remained silent for most of the journey.

However, on the train from Calais to Paris, Holmes, at last, broke his silence.

"Reilly, hopefully our presence will not unduly disturb Anastasia. All we must do is determine that she is well, well cared for and we can then leave knowing the best; which you can then report to Marie and the family on the island.

"I agree."

However, other than the few disturbing words describing Anastasia from Marie, they had no forewarning of the true extent of her mental state.

They were in Paris by mid-afternoon of the third of November and went immediately by Paris taxi to the address that Holmes said was hers.

They ascended the stairs and Reilly knocked on her door. When she opened it and saw Reilly, she screamed in joy and threw her arms around his neck and pulled him in, kissing his cheeks as she did so. Holmes watched warily, followed them in, then closed the door.

"Reilly, Reilly," she kept repeating and kissing his cheeks as he struggled gently to extricate himself from this surprising onslaught of affection. When finally he had done so, still holding her arms tenderly as precaution against another burst of regard, they sat on a little sofa she had placed to catch the northern light.

"You've found me, you've found me. But how?"

Reilly pointed to Holmes.

Anastasia looked confusedly at Holmes, who, as Mr. Stash, slowly removed his eye patch and stood until Anastasia shot upright at her recognition and now Holmes was under her attack of affection.

"Enough, enough, Anastasia. I am happy to see you, too," said Holmes, now trying to disengage as Reilly had just moments before. Reilly sat and laughed.

Suddenly, there was an alarming shift in her personality. She had now become quite perfunctory. The laughter had turned to robotic courtesy.

"Would either of you gentlemen like some tea?"

Reilly and Holmes looked at each other. She was one moment flowing water, the next, solid ice.

"Why yes, if you would be so kind," said Holmes in a most measured and reassuring tone.

"Just do as she says," Holmes said. "She seems to be suffering from a psychosis. I hadn't prepared for this and all is quite delicate at the moment. I think it best we do as she asks and handle her most gingerly."

"We have to get her back to London. If she's gone bonkers there's no telling what she'll say about her family," Reilly whispered.

"I concur. We must bring her to Watson. As a physician, he will have the legal ability to arrange the care she will need."

Reilly nodded in agreement as Anastasia served the tea in a most delicate manner, then sat opposite them.

"Please don't think I'm still not pleased to see you, but one should not be too effusive with one's emotions, should one?"

"I couldn't concur more...effusively" Holmes joked, stressing the word 'effusively' in trying to make her laugh again. It didn't work.

"Sirs," Anastasia said, turning her head from one to the other then back again, "have you come to rescue me?"

"I'm sure you don't need rescuing, Anastasia," Holmes said.

"Yes, I am Anastasia. I am the youngest daughter of Tsar Nicholas II. I am a Grand Duchess."

"Why do you think we've come to rescue you?" Reilly asked.

"Well, you've already done it once. Why not again?"

"Do you feel as though you need to be rescued?" Holmes asked.

"No. Do you?" Anastasia replied.

"Anastasia, we've come from your sisters. We're going to take you to see Marie and Tatiana and Olga," Reilly said.

Suddenly she was joyful again, clapping her hands as she twirled about the studio.

"Oh wonderful, wonderful. What should I wear?" She ran to a bureau and began rummaging through the drawers, tossing garments this way and that.

Holmes intervened to stop this hurricane of clothing.

"Anastasia, we will take care of that. Do you have a valise?" Holmes asked.

"There," Anastasia pointed to a corner cluttered with bric-a-brac and other unimportant objects.

As Anastasia continued her sartorial search, digging like an archaeologist about to uncover an undiscovered Egyptian tomb, Holmes and Reilly agreed that they would take only what would be necessary for the journey back to London.

They managed to have her select that which she wanted to take on her journey to see her sisters and while Holmes helped her put her choices into her valise, Reilly left to fetch a taxi.

In the midst of these simultaneous exertions, Anastasia was singing what sounded like lullabies in Russian, and skipping in excitement around her studio.

Done with the packing, more like pushing and prodding articles into her valise, Holmes gently escorted Anastasia down to the street where Reilly awaited with the taxi.

"Oh, sir, what a beautiful coach. And magical, too, because there are no horses."

"Yes, Anastasia, your footman is holding the coach door open for you."

Reilly gave him Holmes an irritated look but took Anastasia's hand, helping her in, then Holmes and he got in, and he directed the driver to get them to the train station.

It was now a little past five. With luck, they might be able to make the next train back to Calais, then the return ferry to Dover, and finally a late connection back to London. Anastasia still had her British passport as Anna Anders, and so she became Anna Anders once again.

Their luck did, indeed hold, but the journey was fraught with Anastasia's frequent change of demeanor.

On the train from Paris to Calais, she wondered at the scenery and was gratified at all the people bowing to her as she passed. In reality, she was viewing trees swaying in the wind.

On the ferry to Dover, she became a bit seasick and Holmes had to hold her head in his lap and hum to her to calm her jittery stomach. Reilly made a face at Holmes indicating what a lovely picture that made. Holmes, like Queen Victoria, was not amused.

On the train back to London, she would sleep for a moment, awake, yawn, stretch marvel that the moon was out instead of the sun, thinking this midday. She would then nap again and the process would repeat.

It was also on the last part of the journey that Holmes became Mr. Stash once more. All he needed to do was replace the eye patch.

At last, back at Victoria Station, Holmes, holding onto Anastasia's valise, hailed a cab. Reilly was carrying Anastasia in his arms as she slept, and though he received some inquisitive stares at this late hour, his response was, "Drank too much," which seemed to suffice quite nicely.

Holmes helped them in to the cab then closed the door.

"You know I can accompany you no further. You must go to Watson and tend to your charge."

"I know," Reilly said, "I'll report to you as soon as arrangements are made."

"That won't be necessary," Holmes said, "I will know." He then tapped the roof of the cab and at just past midnight, once more Elizabeth and I were awakened by a knocking on my front door.

"Who could that possibly be, at this hour?" Elizabeth asked, quite rightly.

"I'll soon find out," I said as I slipped on my robe and slippers and made my way to the front door.

"Who is there?" I demanded.

"It's me, Reilly. Open the door." He was speaking in loud whispers and until I opened the door I couldn't understand why.

"Good lord, Reilly, what has happened?"

"Who is that, John. Are you all right?" Elizabeth called down from above.

"Yes, Elizabeth, nothing is wrong. Just a slight emergency which I will attend to in my study."

As Elizabeth and I were speaking, Reilly carried Anastasia into my study and set her down on the divan. I closed the door and then I saw Anastasia. True, she was four years older now and not as groomed as before, but I recognised her immediately. I also believe that Reilly had to hold me up, for my knees buckled at the surprise.

"Anastasia! Here? What has happened?"

271

"John, it is very late and since I saw you last I have been to Paris and back to fetch her. May I please have a drink. A rather large drink."

"Of course, of course," I said. "But you must explain."

His large scotch in hand, he proceeded to tell me what, at the time, he was able.

"From what you've said, I must concur that she's mad. But I'm a medical doctor, not a psychiatrist." I said.

"She claims to be exactly who she is," Reilly said, "but since she's supposed to be dead, some people think she's balmy and others think she's genuine. And that's where the danger lies, as you so well know."

"Is that all?" I asked.

"There's more. She drifts from being regal in bearing to acting like the playful Anastasia we knew in Russia and in Eleuthera. But since the death of Alexei, she had been retreating into another world; much like the Tsarina had."

"Not to mean this in jest, but it could quite easily run in the family.

"Reilly, I'm going to need your help. Stay here while I dress. We're going to take her to Maudsley, it's a brand new psychiatric facility in South London. I'm affiliated there, I can admit her, secure a room and then see how she responds in the morning."

"Yes, please, whatever you think best. I'll just sip your scotch, wait and if you could bring me a bite to eat, it would be appreciated. I haven't had the chance to eat much of anything today."

Elizabeth demanded to know why I was going to Maudsley, or anywhere, for that matter, at so advanced an hour. All I could do was tell her the truth, this time. That a very dear friend had brought his "niece" to me for immediate attention and that I felt I had to bring her to Maudsley for proper care. Being a physician's wife, she understood, kissed me on the cheek and reminded me not to awaken her upon my return.

I bought some buttered bread with jam to Reilly, which he consumed eagerly, entirely, and quickly. And then we both carried Anastasia, still asleep, to a cab I flagged.

We arrived at Maudsley at a bit after one a.m., Anastasia still asleep, and I had her admitted immediately as a medical case, not psychiatric.

Seeing that she would be cared for in the best possible manner, Reilly and I stepped outside her room.

"Reilly, let me speak with the attending nurses one more time to be assured all is correct, and then we can leave."

All was most certainly correct and we climbed into a cab which took me to my home.

"John, I'm staying at the Cumberland," Reilly said. "I'll be there until you reach me and let me know about Anastasia. And thank you."

"For what? For helping a young woman in distress and a not-so-young man, as well?" I said this in jest, of course.

"I'll remember that." He patted me on the shoulder and I got out. The cab drove away. It was now almost four in the morning.

Upon waking at about ten, Reilly sent a coded message to Tatiana that he had found Anastasia, that they were back in London, that she was well, and being cared for; that he had seen Marie, that she was well, too, and that he would send more information when he could.

At about noon, Reilly rang Marie and asked her to meet him at that same bench in about an hour, if possible. It was and she did and she appeared most anxious to learn of her sister.

"Marie, Anastasia is here. She's safe."

"Oh, thank heaven. And thank you, Reilly." She gave him a hug.

"Stop that, Marie, people will report this to William." She laughed then saw he had something else to say.

"Yes, there is more. Marie, that odd state that you'd described to me, about Anastasia, well it may be that she has a sort of psychosis."

"What's that?"

"She may be mentally unbalanced."

"My god, where is she?"

"I can't tell you, as yet. I, myself am waiting to hear how she's doing. But I can assure you that she's in the best of medical hands. There's no one outside of our family who could care for her more."

"Dr. Watson. She's with Dr. Watson."

"Yes. He has her at a facility where they'll be able to study her for a few days and determine what she may be suffering from. But once again, Dr. Watson is at her side and she's safe."

"All right. At least I have that. I'll wait to hear from you again. Oh, I should've asked before, is it all right for me to call you Reilly or do you have another name now?"

He told her.

"Windsor? Roland Windsor?"

"Don't ask."

Reilly And I Meet For The Last Time?

In three days, I was able to leave word for Reilly and we met in the bar at the Cumberland.

"It's rather interesting news, Reilly. She's been examined by a group of excellent psychiatrists and their diagnoses concur.

"On the positive side, she's suffering under a benign delusion and can function rather normally. However, on the negative side, she's reverted to a semi-childlike condition and as one of the psychiatrists put it rather colloquially, she might be "an easy mark".

"There's also a prognosis that as she ages, she'll do as Merlin did and "youthen"; that is she'll become intellectually younger and younger."

"So what do they say can be done?"

"Nothing right now. She's an English citizen, physically quite healthy, as I attested, and she should be permitted to live her life as she chooses."

"So she's to be set free?"

"Yes, in two days, in fact. Yesterday I was able to lease a very nice flat for her. I'll see that she's moved in and settled. Don't worry about that.

"I just wish I had a way of looking after her on a daily basis."

"Don't worry. I may have an answer for that," Reilly said.

"I know better than to ask what; but I also know it will be done."

"Now, how many times in these last few years have I said that we'll probably never see each other again; and each time been proved so terribly wrong?" Reilly asked.

"Too many." We both gave a knowing chuckle and he extended his hand.

"I won't say it this time," Reilly said.

We stood, shook hands, and I returned home.

A little while later, in a quite different part of London, Reilly had another reunion.

"Again? You're here again?" Holmes asked as Reilly came through his office door, guided up the steps by one of the usual.

"I promised I'd let you know about Anastasia and that's what I'm here for."

Holmes listened carefully and then said, "Yes. As before, I can have someone watch her. It will be done."

"Holmes, will you ever become yourself again?"

"I'm exploring new and unconquered worlds here. And Watson must always be safe."

"But Holmes, the danger is passed. The men will never trouble Watson or his family."

"But we cannot be sure, can we?"

After a moment's pause, "No, we cannot." But he knew that Holmes was using this as an excuse.

"So come and join me. Become me. Holmes became Clay. Reilly can become Clay."

"No, Holmes, no."

Holmes said no more. He simply shrugged in his chair then stood and shook hands with Reilly; who then went back down those stairs.

And as I write this, I never saw Reilly again. He was correct this time.

The U.S. Marines Sent In

However, I did hear from someone, or rather, two, who had heard from Reilly. Two American Marine majors, Lou and Martin Curtis.

In January of 1942, right after Pearl Harbor, they showed up at my home and were very happy to meet "the celebrated Dr. John Watson;" of course, a very good way of beginning a conversation with me.

It seemed their father, Hank, had given them a package from a close friend of his, to deliver to me and to one else but me. In their American military G-2 parlance, it was an "eyes only" package. And quite a thick one, at that.

I asked who this friend was, and they said they didn't know. "Remember," Martin said, "it's eyes only; your eyes."

"Yeah," Lou said, "we're just the feet."

They then explained they needed to leave since there was a meeting to attend at the Admiralty. I thanked them both for their trouble; not knowing who they were until I read what was inside. They gave me a proper U.S. Marine salute and were on their way.

I prayed for their safety as I did daily for my son, John, the newest Dr. Watson, serving in North Africa; and for all the boys and men from all the countries fighting with us against the Nazis.

What I found when I looked inside quite gave me a start. It was a note from Reilly and a packet of papers detailing the very brief summary in the note. I had not heard one word from him since that day in November of 1924.

This is what his note said:

January 14, 1942
Dear Dr. Watson, John,

It's been a very long time. About twenty years. And now we're in another war with the same enemy. Isn't this where we came in?

I'm writing now because you should know more about what happened with Holmes.

The pages included in this package, will explain all, and I trust that our government have

more to worry about than something that happened during the last war.

I'm sorry I couldn't have been more forthcoming when we were together in London, but after reading, I think you'll understand.

At this time in our nation's history, the truth should be told; which I know you'll do because you're incapable of doing otherwise.

All is well here, and all send their love.

R

Then after reading the pages he had sent, and which you've just read woven into his verbal narrative with me, what was I to believe; what Reilly was telling me now, or what he had told me before?

My greatest sorrow, however, was never to truly know if Holmes was dead or alive; no matter what Reilly had told me.

I suspected that if Holmes were alive, he would have devised some secure way in which to inform me. But had I known the truth, would I have let the truth out in error? Had Holmes been alive, might that have endangered him further?

But as I said at the very beginning of this, "this is a retelling of a tale previously told by someone to someone else expert in tailoring tales to his taste. Which, in itself, is a sentence needing elucidation by Holmes."

I shall leave it to him.

John H. Watson, M.D.

February 2, 1942

Final Secrets Revealed And New Surprises

Having finished, I glanced at my watch, but then remembered Sidney had taken it. I had no idea what time it was or how long I'd been reading.

I sat for a few moments, once more looking at my grandfather's words and running my fingers over his handwriting so I could feel as if I were actually touching him. How I missed him.

But as always, other questions arose and once again, I knew that only Sidney could answer them.

I slowly pushed the chair away from the desk, stood and stretched. I then went looking for Sidney, and found him in the room next door, sitting and sipping a brandy.

"Well, John. Once again it seems I've brought you and your grandfather together. Come sit, have a brandy with me."

This I did immediately and then began firing questions at Sidney as quickly as they would come out of my mouth. The first was, "Where's my watch and what time is it?"

"Here's your watch," he said as he handed it to me and you tell the time yourself."

It was a tad passed midnight.

"Now you can begin your inquisition in earnest," Sidney laughed.

"Okay. Did Holmes live or was the whole thing a something your father invented?"

"I'm afraid you'd have to ask him; but since he's deceased, that might pose a problem. But yes, it seems that

Holmes did live. But as you've just read, Holmes never contacted your grandfather to protect him.

"John, if what was written is true, then Holmes had become what he and your grandfather had fought against all those years before; and, I believe, was Holmes was so shamed by it that he would not sully your grandfather's presence with his own."

"So he never saw my grandfather again?"

"I didn't say that. Though this is only based on idle innuendo from people who might have known, it seems that Holmes saw your grandfather rather frequently, but not in a reciprocal manner.

"It's said that Holmes spent many a night as guardian angel in shadow view of your grandfather's home. It's even said that one night, when a thief tried to enter the home, he was done in by Holmes who had his men drag the man away. He looked once more at the house, turned back into the fog and the night, never to see his dearest friend again.

"Mind you, it's only mere blather.

"As to your grandparents, as far as I knew, my father never saw them again, nor did he ever contact your grandfather again once he had returned to Eleuthera. Except for that letter and package of papers.

"As to what happened to the rest of my family, that in itself is quite a tale."

"Please, Sidney, That's something I really need to know," I said.

"My grandfather, the Tsar, perhaps overburdened with the fact that his beloved Russia was once again being viciously attacked by the Germans, passed away quietly on Eleuthera at the outset of WWII. He's buried between Alexandra and Alexei, according to his wishes.

"My father and mother lived happily there until their own death by natural causes in the early 1960s; although my father had to return to London quite frequently. They're buried in the same area as the others.

"Anastasia, having drifted into madness, spent the rest of her life trying to convince the world she was truly who she said she was; although for whatever reason, she never mentioned our family.

"Later on, after WWII, although she didn't realize it, she was tended to by
Dr. Lasker, the doctor on Eleuthera after your father left. She died in London, living as late as 1979. I had anonymously supplied the funds for her care in her later life at Maudsley, in South London. I'm sure you know it."

"Of course, I do. My grandfather was affiliated there and would, on a regular..." I stopped speaking because a bright light had just turned on in my memory and literally gave me goose bumps.

"Now that makes sense," I said. "My grandfather would visit a woman he said was an old friend and he was just looking in on her, checking up on her well-being. He did this on a fairly regular basis. Being affiliated there, he was able to converse with the other doctors and he continued to visit for as long as he was physically able."

"I know," Sidney said.

"You know? How?"

"Because I saw him there, from time to time. Of course, he never saw me, or if he did he wouldn't have known who I was. But every so often as I was leaving Aunt Anastasia, or just arriving, I'd see your grandfather either exiting her room or, if they were conversing in a lounge, I'd wait for him to leave before visiting her."

I just shook my head at how fate kept its chessboard pieces moving about.

"If my deepest memory serves, Sidney, I seem to have a very slight memory of my grandfather once taking me to visit this very special friend of his.

"I think I was about five and, wait, now that I remember; it was my father who took me, not my grandfather. He had already passed. My father held my hand. I'm remembering now. We went to a lounge there and my father sat next to a small old woman…"

Sidney interrupted. "Yes, she was small, but she was only about fifty-eight when you saw her. But then again, any woman with white hair would seem like an old woman to a boy of only five."

"Yes, she had white hair and I remember my father saying, "John, I'd like you meet a very special friend of mine. A real-life princess. Her name is Anna.""

"Well to a boy of five, princesses were young and beautiful and had long blonde hair and they most certainly did not look like this Anna person. But I remember that I bowed to her, which made her laugh.

"She extended her hand to me and I kissed it. That really made her laugh. Then she withdrew her hand and rubbed it on her dress to rub off the moisture from my kiss.

"I think that's it, I don't seem to remember any more."

"Well, let's see if this refreshes your memory. Do you remember a man giving you a treat and saying, 'All boys who are nice to princesses get treats?'"

It took a second and then a bigger light went off.

"It was you?"

"Yes. That was me. I had been watching from across the lounge that day, and couldn't resist making contact with two generations of Watsons, when your grandfather meant so much to the Romanovs."

I felt myself tearing up; it was such a beautiful story. Then I remembered that he hadn't told me about his little sister.

"Sidney, what about Alix?"

"My younger sister Alix moved to Los Angeles when she turned eighteen,
just before the war started for the Americans. Incredibly, she became a famous Hollywood movie star of the 1950s and 1960s, but I won't say who she was."

Though I didn't say anything to Sidney, I thought to myself, "I hope she didn't meet Bugsy Siegel out there. It would've been too tragically ironic."

Sidney continued.

"Of course, no one knew who she really was. Or is. She still lives there. I even escorted her once to one of those big Hollywood premieres. You know the ones; with those gigantic searchlights crisscrossing the sky and screaming fans shredding their larynxes.

"Alix loved the idolatry but I found it disconcerting."

I desperately tried to pry the secret out of Sidney of who Alix really was but got nowhere. We both laughed when I said that she's probably the only movie queen who could've been a real one, as well.

As for Sidney himself, he told me he'd been educated in England and chose to reside in London for his entire life, only occasionally returning to visit his family. And upon their passing, never went back to Eleuthera. He would only tell me that his family name was most certainly not Reilly.

"And what of your grandparents, John?" Sidney asked. "While I heard about them, from time to time, and I had that little moment with the two Watson men at Maudsley, I never introduced myself. I felt it might be too jarring and certainly didn't want to call attention to who I was.

I told Sidney of my grandmother's passing during WWII, and of my grandfather following when I was about six. He told me that he had read about the death of both, and had quietly attended my grandfather's funeral.

I told him of my father's bedtime stories about Holmes and my grandfather, and of how my grandfather never let a day pass without this tiny prayer, "Safe home, Holmes. Wherever you are."

Then shifting my train of thought, I said, "My Lord, Sidney, I wonder what really did happen to Holmes?"

"Well, to be perfectly frank, I'm not sure. It seems Holmes got his ultimate, twisted wish as your grandfather recounted. He became Clay and disappeared."

"That's it? No one ever hear from him again?" I asked.

"Well…"

"Sidney, you're holding something back. You know what happened."

"John, you're like family to me, so I'll share one other secret with you. Are you sure you want to hear this; because it might be very unsettling."

"Go on, Sidney." I leaned forward eager to hear what he had to say.

"John, remember when Holmes wanted my father to step into his shoes?"

I nodded.

"Unfortunately, the Romanov fortune ran out when the Depression ran in; for my family on Eleuthera as well as Marie in London, although Marie was taken care of by William, at first.

"My father, being an ultimate realist, knew something had to be done so he went to see Holmes again."

"No!"

"Oh, yes," Sidney said and laughed. "By that time, Prohibition was over and the pipeline established by the men in New York and Holmes continued to flow, but legally. And the monies that those men made during Prohibition were then put to use in legitimate businesses. Of course there were still other illegitimate ones, as well.

"By this time, with advanced age, Holmes had no desire to continue as Clay, or Mr. Stash, or whomever. He wanted to be whomever he wanted to be whenever he wanted to be whoever he wanted to be."

I thought of my grandfather's words I'd just read, about someone telling someone else about something or other, or whatever he said. My head had been swimming from my grandfather's ledger, and now what Sidney was telling me made my head feel like Mt. Etna.

"Sidney, as Siegel said, please peak English." Sidney laughed again.

"It's really quite simple. When Holmes had had enough, it coincided perfectly with our family not having enough; so my father became Holmes-Clay-Stash and took over the international network, continuing to work with Lansky and Luciano and Siegel.

"And when my father had had enough, I became Reilly-Holmes-Clay-Stash. It was only recently that I relinquished my reins to the son of one of my father's closest and most trusted friends. Someone whose father met with a fatal accident in Helsinki."

"No..."

"Yes. Yrjö's son, Timo.

"On his first trip back to London to take over from Holmes, my father made it a point of finding Yrjö. As it turned out, he was living in London, this was now 1948, I believe, so on my father's frequent trips there, he and Yrjö would always meet to talk about old times and to hoist a few.

"Of course my father would brag about me and Yrjö would brag about Timo.

"For whatever reason, Yrjö would return to Helsinki on a regular basis. I suspect he might still have been SIS and had a hand in all that Cold War spy stuff.

"It was on one such trip that he died, in 1952. Timo was only four at the time. His mother had died giving birth, which was common at that time after the war.

"Poor Timo. From that point on, my father paid for his education, his clothing, everything; and he came to regard my father as his own, and me, as an uncle.

"When he was old enough, I trained him to be my successor, just as my father had trained me."

I just sat there dumbfounded.

"John, you've seen my cars, you've seen parts of this one particular home, do you think luxury such as I possess came from...where, the tooth fairy?"

"But that's incredible!"

"To say the least."

"I just thought you had invested wisely over the years."

"My father invested globally, yes; if that's the term you'd like to use.

"He invested in distilleries, in trucking companies which were legitimate but also were able to transport illicit substances; in garbage and waste disposal; in the burgeoning businesses being developed after the war; and in controlling the unions that controlled almost everything, at that time.

"He also invested in Hollywood motion picture studios; and, yes, that opened doors for Alix,

"But most of all, in gambling casinos all over the world. Especially in Havana and a little town you may have heard of, Las Vegas."

"Las Vegas?"

"Brace yourself. I'm not sure if you're aware of this, but it was Bugsy Siegel who invented Las Vegas."

"I've heard about that but never paid it any mind."

"Well you should've, John, you should've; because that is one true-life fairy tale.

"Siegel had gone out to Hollywood in the Thirties, sent there by Luciano and Lansky to watch over the gambling and the motion picture companies that they were moving into. He already had an old friend out there from New York who had become a movie star, George Raft.

"Funny, Raft was not a gangster in New York; just a hoofer and a man who had grown up with Siegel; but he was the one who played tough gangsters in the movies.

"Anyway, Siegel was driving through the desert of Nevada back to Hollywood when he stopped in a little nothing called Las Vegas. He needed gas, food, and then he saw the cheap casinos. As they say, the proverbial light bulb went off brighter than an exploding nova.

"He built the first true luxury hotel and casino out there, the Flamingo, financed by the usual group. But the costs kept going up and up and the partners back in New York smelled something, shall we say, not kosher.

"Lansky went out there personally to reason with Siegel, to warn him that if the hotel didn't make back the millions they poured into it, and very soon, he might be poured into the cornerstone of the next hotel.

"Siegel assured him all was okay and that the opening would be the greatest opening in the history of openings. It was a dud.

"To this day, nobody knows who did it and the case as never been solved, but Siegel was shot through those big blue eyes of his one night at his home."

"Sidney, how do you know about all this?"

"I was twenty-eight. I was there. My father had suggested I learn the business from the bottom up when I was still in my teens and I had always been a crack shot when I was in the Royal Marines."

"Are you saying...?" He cut me off.

"John, I don't know what you may be assuming, but I assume it's incorrect. "However, if one's younger sister is deflowered by a psychopathic killer, one must take appropriate action."

It added up. Alix had met Siegel out in Hollywood and the unthinkable happened. If the men back in New York wanted a certain action taken on a partner who had been stealing from the men who steal, who better to take that action than a family member; both literally and figuratively.

"However," Sidney continued, "my father stayed partners with Meyer and Charlie until he passed. And when he did in 1961 they asked me to take over the family business, so-to-speak.

"Which I did, of course and stayed partners with Meyer and Charlie until they died of natural causes; Charlie by a heart attack in Naples in 1962 and Meyer in Miami Beach, in 1983."

I sat there very quietly, seeing Sidney in an entirely altered plane. The dear, sweet old man with all the secrets, appeared now a cold, cunning old killer with even greater secrets.

"But you have nothing to fear, John. As I've said, you're family. I've told you these secrets because you are family. Do you understand?" He said this calmly, quietly, with a modicum of menace.

"I believe so, Sidney."

"Good. I'll pour some more brandy."

"Sidney, what about you? Didn't you ever marry?"

As soon as I asked, I could see memories carrying him away from our room and into his past. His face reflected such a radiant happiness, and then he was back.

"Yes, yes. I was married. Once. But she died tragically and I wish not to discuss it."

I felt terrible about the question and paused for a moment. Then I remembered that some people had not been accounted for and felt it might brighten him again.

"Sidney, what about Marie and William? You left out Marie and William."

"Oh, my Aunt Marie and Uncle William led a very happy life until WWII. "Unfortunately, William, who'd risen to flag rank, was commanding the heavy cruiser *Norfolk* during the battle to sink the Bismarck in May of '41, and was killed during that battle.

"Marie was, of course, devastated; but luckily and happily, remarried a few years later; a very nice man, Ethan Cooper. He owned a profitable group of electronics shops across the U.K.

"And although it was later in life and quite dangerous at that time, Marie gave birth to a healthy, little girl. Marie passed away peacefully here in England in October of 1976, Ethan in 1980.

"From what I understand, the girl was never informed of who her mother really was; of course, for her own protection. And the financial comfort she enjoyed came from the income from her father's business. As I mentioned before, Marie's original funds had long ago run out.

"And what about her? What happened to Marie's daughter?" I asked.

"Oh, her?" Sidney asked, as he pointed to a silver-framed photo on the table next to me.

I looked at the photo carefully and then had to look again, uncomprehending.

I stammered, "But this is a picture of my wife, Joan."

About the Author

Phil Growick has been a Sherlock Holmes fan since he watched a black and white Basil Rathbone and Nigel Bruce on his grandparents' TV when he was five.

The Revenge of Sherlock Holmes is the sequel to his first Holmes book, *The Secret Journal Of Dr. Watson* - It has a surprise ending that no one, as yet, expected; and left everyone demanding to know what happened to all the major characters; primarily, of course, Holmes.

Growick is the Managing Director of The Howard Sloan Koller Group in New York City, recruiting for the top, international advertising talent. If you like a great TV commercial, chances are the people who created it are represented by him.

His advertising books are *My First Time*, and *My First Time W*.

His greatest joys are his wife, his sons, his daughter-in-law, and his grandson.

Also from Phil Growick

"Phil Growick's, 'The Secret Journal of Dr Watson', is an adventure which takes place in the latter part of Holmes and Watson's lives. They are entrusted by HM Government (although not officially) and the King no less to undertake a rescue mission to save the Romanovs, Russia's Royal family from a grisly end at the hand of the Bolsheviks. There is a wealth of detail in the story but not so much as would detract us from the enjoyment of the story. Espionage, counter-espionage, the ace of spies himself, double-agents, double-crossers...all these flit across the pages in a realistic and exciting way. All the characters are extremely well-drawn and Mr Growick, most importantly, does not falter with a very good ear for Holmesian dialogue indeed. The tale is fantastic yes, but the skill of the author is apparent for he makes us believe that these events could have happened just as he describes. None of the content is superfluous in any way at all and the whole is a pleasure to read. Highly recommended. A five-star effort."
The Baker Street Society

Also published in Italian, Russian, and audio versions.

Also from MX Publishing

MX Publishing is the world's largest specialist Sherlock Holmes publisher, with over a hundred and fity titles and sixty authors creating the latest in Sherlock Holmes fiction and non-fiction.

The collections includes traditional short story collections and novels through to travel guides and quiz books.

Our leading biography titles include the #1 bestseller *Benedict Cumberbatch In Transition* and *The Norwood Author* which won the 2011 Howlett Award (Sherlock Holmes Book of the Year).

Join our Facebook page for the latest Sherlock Holmes book news. www.facebook.com/BooksSherlockHolmes

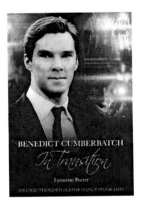

www.mxpublishing.co.uk (UK)

www.mxpublishing.com (USA)

CPSIA information can be obtained at www.ICGtesting.com
Printed in the USA
LVOW12s0428050614

388586LV00003B/157/P